The Report

Also by Jessica Francis Kane

Bending Heaven

The Report

Jessica Francis Kane

Portobello
BOOKS

Published by Portobello Books 2011

Portobello Books
12 Addison Avenue
London
W11 4QR

First published in the United States by Graywolf Press, Minneapolis,
Minnesota.

A CIP catalogue record is available from the British Library.

9 8 7 6 5 4 3 2 1

ISBN 978 1 84627 279 0

www.portobellobooks.com

Offset by Avon DataSet Ltd, Bidford on Avon, Warwickshire

Printed in the UK by CPI William Clowes Beccles NR34 7TL

For Mitchell

"We want to note what we have done, and not done."

—Preface, *The 9/11 Commission Report*

"When hope is lost, blame is the only true religion."

—John Burnham Schwartz, *Reservation Road*

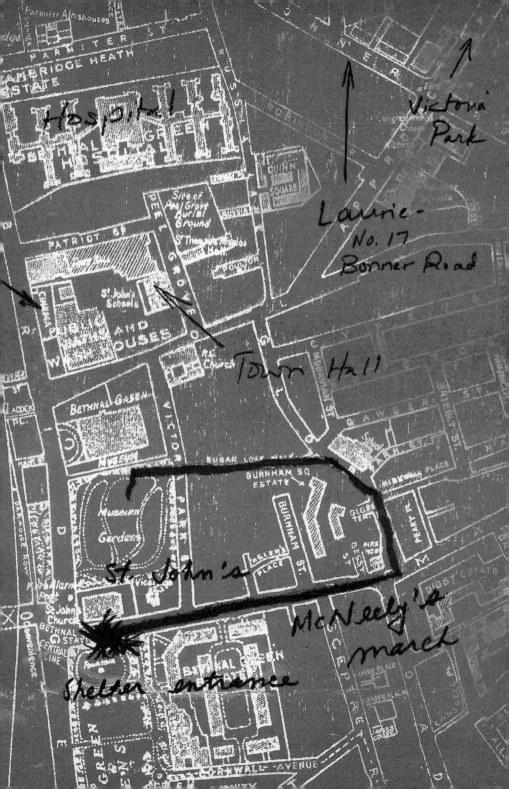

THESE SECTIONS ARE CLOSED

PILLAR

BOOKING HALL

59 STEPS DOWN TO
PLATFORM AND SHELTER

PILLAR

CENTRAL LINE

VICTORIA
LINE

LANDING

NATIONAL MEMORIAL

FLIGHT

FLIGHT

ENTRANCE
TO SHELTER

SCALE ~ 10' to 1".

Edwards
(Henderson)

Hastings } office
Low

STREET LEVEL

FIRST LANDING LEV.

BOOKING HALL LEV.

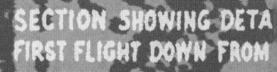

1½"

WOODEN FRONTS.

SECTION SHOWING DETA
FIRST FLIGHT DOWN FROM

19 STEPS DOWN TO LANDING   LANDING 15' × 10'

7 STEPS DOWN TO
BOOKING HALL

7' × 4"

HANDRAIL

LIGHT

7' 9"

Low

Bagshaw
Steadman

Contents

Retrospective

Begin with the retrospective.

On an overcast evening in early March, after the weather forecast, a television special about the tragedy at Bethnal Green begins. In a sonorous voice a narrator describes the underground shelters, the unseasonably cold weather of March 1943, the psychological effects of long-term aerial bombardment. The camera pans over a series of images of wartime Bethnal Green, and several survivors speak, a man named Bill Steadman among the most compelling. His face ruddy from high blood pressure, he talks about receiving the babies. "Greatest thing I've ever done," he says. "I've tried to live the rest of my life as though it meant something. Why else was I there?"

It is the thirtieth anniversary of the tragedy. Not to the day. That would have been 3 March, last Saturday, but various television authorities felt the retrospective would do better during the week, so Wednesday, 7 March, it is. The weather is cold, snow beginning to mix with rain, though the weather report failed to mention it. At Paddington trains slow, and on Oxford Street a bus stalls, impeding the evening commute in several directions. By eight o'clock, however, most problems clear, and people continue home.

When the programme is over, Tilly Barber switches off her set. She's eight years older than the tragedy and remembers it well. Thin and strong, she looks like a survivor, though she does not think of herself that way. She stands a minute, then instinctively begins to move towards her boys. They're not far away; the flat is small, though with two bedrooms and everything she needs behind her own door, it's the most space she's ever had. When she sees that the two are sleeping soundly, their small backs rising and falling, she opens the boys' door wide and begins to cry.

She misses her mother, to whom, after the accident, she was never kind. She can still hear Ada's question when Tilly was pregnant the first time, "If you have a girl, do you think you'd call her Emma?"

"No, Mum," she answered, surprised by the need she still felt to hold her mother accountable. "I don't think I would."

Tilly closes the door and starts to get ready for bed herself. She runs a hand through her cropped hair, folds her clothes, and puts them in a neat pile on a chair in the corner. She can't wait for the time when this story will no longer be alive for her. She wants to be able to look back on it, see its beginning, middle, and end. Laurence Dunne tried to give her family an ending—she understands that now—but she shuts her eyes against the idea. Tilly has held on to the truth, the hardest thing she's ever done. She hopes one day to be able to say in simple summary, "It was a difficult time," and be done with it, but she isn't there yet, and so she says very little at all.

Shelter

One

When the cinema went dark, the audience stirred into life. People leaned towards the shapes in the seats next to them. "What happened?" they asked. "Did you see?"

The film stars had been arguing, a humorous disagreement because they didn't know they were in love. The heroine was *feisty*, a popular word of the time, 1943, though the people of London were exhausted, grimy, numb. Clean and feisty existed only in American movies; that's why they were adored and why the Museum Cinema that night in Bethnal Green was full. People were standing along the walls and sitting cross-legged in the aisles.

The hero of the film had just turned and lifted his hands. There had been some kind of movement. Did he cup her face? Put his hands in her hair?

"Did you see?"

Several boys switched on torches, and when the voices began to subside, the cinema manager, walking up to the stage, said the usual bit: the alert had sounded; if you wish to leave, please do so quietly.

Someone in front shouted, "Never mind! Put the film back on!"

The manager sighed. Four films had shown through the previous night after a large portion of the audience refused to leave. He stared a moment, remembering the fish-and-chip mess he'd faced in the cinema that morning and the puffy, sleepless face of his youngest projectionist. Tonight he wanted the crowd to go.

"If you wish to leave, please do so quietly," he said again.

The audience stayed, the torchlight settled. There wasn't much incentive to go. The cinemas were fairly good shelters and the dark wasn't a problem; they'd all been living under the rules of blackout for years. Their homes, behind boarded windows, could be oppressive, but the darkness of the streets or shelters or cinemas, especially on the night of a raid, was a world they understood. When the ice-cream seller opened the back door, however, which let in the siren's wail, people began to move.

It had been a beautiful afternoon, though later no one would remember that. A football match in the Museum Gardens had drawn a large crowd, and when the young borough engineer won the game with an impossible header, people heard the cheer in Stepney. Afterwards a group gathered outside the pub on Russia Lane (affectionately known as the Plots & Pints because of the neighbouring cemetery). The air felt thinner, cleaner, partly because it was—a six-week break in the raids had given the dust and smoke of broken, smouldering buildings time to clear—and partly because the sun was making a rare appearance, polishing the winter-weary houses and trees.

Ada covered her ears before the siren could reach its peak. All afternoon in her shop the women had talked about Monday's bombing of Berlin. The heaviest air raid so far, they said. So many bombs, German farmers saw the fires a hundred miles away. Tonight seemed to them a likely time for the enemy's response, but Ada prayed they were wrong.

She lowered her hands, aware that her girls were watching her. Tilly, eight, had dark half-moons beneath her eyes. Emma, nearly four, had lost weight. Neither girl looked well, even though half an hour before the blackout, she'd taken them out to breathe the fresh tar fumes on the new portion of Jersey Street. All the mothers were talking of the reprisal, of what the new high explosives could do. Before dinner Ada had put two jumpers in her bag and the extra blanket by the front door. The new bombs, the women said, would leave less time to get to the shelter.

Tilly spoke first. "We'd better go."

Ada hurried them from the table and helped them into their winter coats. She pulled Tilly's collar up around her neck, and Tilly winced. "I just want you to stay warm," Ada said.

"I know."

"I'll try to get us something at the canteen," Ada offered, and the girls glanced at each other. That meant she had money, and if she had money, they might be able to get a bunk. They weren't registered for one, but sometimes that didn't matter, depending on the wardens. It was much better to have a bunk in the tunnel than a mat on the platform or tracks.

"Can we bring something to eat and get a bunk instead?" Tilly asked.

"You've just finished dinner!" Ada knew it hadn't been much. She'd served broth and fried potatoes, nothing else, for the third night in a row. She planned to surprise them, though, when they got to the shelter. She had two pieces of chocolate in her pocket. "Now go!"

"We'll play draughts," Tilly whispered to Emma as they went out. She rubbed her sister's hand.

"Can I be black?"

"Of course." Tilly squeezed her. "And if we get a bunk, you can have the pillow."

Emma was impressed. Her sister had let her have the black draughts last time, too, and so she solemnly promised to let Tilly have the pillow.

As Ada locked the door, the girls waited behind her; then the three joined the stream of people pouring out of the tenements that formed the low and boxy skyline of the borough. Ada had moved to Jersey Street when she married, but she and her husband, Robby, like many young couples in Bethnal Green, had grown up only a few streets away. They lived in a row of Victorian terraced houses chopped up into tiny three-room flats—kitchen, living room, bedroom—two flats upstairs, two downstairs. Their stove and toilet were on the landing, shared only with Mr. Levin, across the hall. On the ground floor they kept a greengrocer's, Barber's. "Proof you can escape your name," Robby often joked.

Ada looked down the street, which was quickly growing more crowded. She wondered if Robby would come for them or if he would head straight to the shelter from the Plots & Pints. Several pale faces bobbed forwards against the dark tide.

"Your father will meet us there," Ada said brightly, hoping Robby wouldn't have had too much to drink.

"We should have set out sooner," Tilly said, scanning the crowd. "There are a lot of people tonight, Mum."

Emma started to cry, and Ada picked her up. "Don't pay any attention," she said. "We're fine. Let's count the faces. Do you want to?"

"No," Tilly said.

"How?" asked Emma.

"See how bright they look in the dusk, with everyone else walking the other way? A little ghostly. We could count them."

Nothing about this reassured the girls, and Ada gave up. They liked to be quiet, and she knew she often tried too hard to distract them with games and stories. She was never at her best when she was out alone with them. Before Emma was born she'd managed all right, but her mother had urged her to have another baby. Two hands, two sides, two children, she'd said. Ada wasn't convinced, and when Emma was born, she'd felt the strain immediately. It's just the time, people told her, 1939, war just declared. Then her mother died, and Ada was overwhelmed with the business of running the shop and caring for two children. Tilly was an enormous help, but Ada worried she relied on her too much.

"Mum," Tilly said. "Your slippers?"

Ada looked down and saw that she was walking in her slippers. She forced herself to laugh. "I'll be more comfortable in the shelter. Next time you'll be begging to bring yours."

Ada was glad to see Tilly smile. When was the last time Tilly had laughed? Ada couldn't remember. When she thought of Tilly, the first image that came to mind was a frown of concentration. She touched her daughter's shoulder. "You have slippers, don't you?"

Tilly shook her head. "They're too small."

At the corner of Jersey Street and the Bethnal Green Road, Ada spotted Martin Henderson speaking to a group of boys. It was a comfort to see a constable, and Ada put Emma down and called his name. Martin acknowledged her but was preoccupied with the boys, all of whom were holding torches, one of them lit, a blackout violation.

"Look," Ada said, "it's Constable Henderson. Everything's going to be fine."

She waved as she passed, and Emma, taking her mother's hand on one side, her sister's on the other, blinked away her tears.

The crowd from the cinema filed out slowly along the worn red carpet, and it seemed to Bertram Lodge, at the end of a row and alone, that everyone was holding hands, touching shoulders, whispering. Twenty-two years old, Bertram was a clerk in the town hall and not at the front because of his flat feet. He lived on St. Jude's Road, in a small flat he shared secretly with Clare Newbury, an artist and a nurse, who had gone ahead to the shelter to sketch. Thinking he might join her there now, he stood up and concentrated on the shoes of the girl in front of him, a sleepy girl who kept leaning on the shoulder of a blond boy so that she could lift and twirl her foot whenever the crowd halted. The soles of her shoes were lime green, beautiful and astonishing. How was it that the government forbade the making of trousers with cuffs or pockets or buttons, yet the soles of shoes could be this colour? Bertram thought it must have something to do with surpluses.

They moved into the damaged, dingy lobby, past the gold-painted ticket stall, already abandoned (the proprietor notoriously nervous), and out of the doors on to Cambridge Heath Road. Everyone knew it was Cambridge Heath, though the street sign had been removed at the start of the war, just as everyone knew, despite the ban on weather reports, that it had rained during the film. The pavement was damp. The sky was clear again now, as it had been most of the day, and the Thames was at low ebb. At the beginning of the war, they would look up, searching for planes, delighted to see stars. Now they understood that a clear night with a full moon was dangerous, and they were quiet.

It was a Wednesday, so birds and flowers had been for sale that morning at the stalls along the Bethnal Green Road. Brisk business pleased the traders, but many customers wanted to know when the violets and daffodils would arrive. The traders shook their heads and referred them to the home secretary, Herbert S. Morrison, the only person in England who could lift the ban on flower transport by rail. Until he did so, most of the spring flowers would remain hostage in Wales.

Nevertheless, the *Times* and the *Daily Herald* had run their usual chipper beginning-of-the-month stories that morning, various bright predictions and tallies: pastels popular for spring (dusty pink and leaf green), seventy-eight hours of sunshine last month, and 252 Londoners killed or missing in enemy raids. This monthly total was lower than usual, and yet the numbers had become nearly meaningless, everyone simply marking them as more or less in order to endure the truth.

"Boys," Constable Henderson began severely. The boys froze. Henderson reached down and took the lit torch. He switched it off, then stood, feet apart, slapping the end of it in his palm.

The stance seemed ominous, but if the boys had observed more closely, they might have noticed the sag in Henderson's shoulders, the extra weight around his middle, the puffiness under his eyes, and they would have realized they had little to fear. Henderson was tired, not yet ready for his evening patrol, and feeling grim about the night's probable direction. According to protocol he was due at the shelter entrance as soon as possible after the alert, but he felt he should give the boys a lecture and was summoning the strength. Many evacuated children had recently returned to the area, yet most of the schools were closed. Reports of petty crime were on the rise; a looting gang was working in the area. And then there were the refugees, groups of quiet people who seemed to wait for something no one could give them. What had started slowly before the war—a few children here, a family there—had accelerated. Now places where his friends had once congregated or shopped were often full of strangers. Everyone said they needed time, they'd suffered horribly. Thus it had become customary to help the refugees while expecting them to change soon, an unsatisfactory arrangement for all. It made Henderson rub his forehead. Someone needed to start cracking down, he thought, and so he delayed his arrival at the shelter to speak to the boys.

Bertram, the young clerk, followed the quick licks of green in front of him, wondering if Clare would like a pair of shoes like that. He had just bought her a new sketchbook, but as he was always giving her those, it didn't feel like a proper present. She'd been drawing when they met, in the Museum Gardens at the beginning of the war. Her posture and steady concentration had made him think she must be very talented. He walked behind her to see the scene from her perspective, and that was when he discovered two things: she drew poorly, and the main object of her attention was not a tree, as he'd assumed, but a dead woman caught upside down in its branches. Blown there by one of the bombs the night before. Torn by shrapnel.

The sound that escaped him stopped her hand, and Clare looked up. Then they both turned back to the dead woman. Part of the scalp was dangling off, but her long blond hair glowed in the sun.

"Why are you drawing?" Bertram managed.

She told him that since the bombing had started, people had spent a lot of time saying, "It's unimaginable," but she thought they meant, "I hadn't imagined it before this."

Her blue eyes steady and dry, she said, "I will. I'll draw and remember and I won't be surprised again."

He nodded and sat down beside her until she finished.

Now Bertram turned left with everyone else towards the corner and the Bethnal Green Road. He smiled when he saw the petals and loose feathers the evening rain had pinned in the gutters and was happy for the company of the crowd. In spite of the siren, no one seemed rushed or worried.

Two

The young man on the step had olive skin that blushed copper. When the door opened, he clenched his jaw, which he knew to be square and handsome. He didn't look English—he knew that too—but he prided himself on his nearly perfect Oxbridge accent.

"Sir Laurence," he said. "I'm Paul Barber. I wrote to you about the thirtieth anniversary of the Bethnal Green report?"

The man in the doorway stood firm.

"I hope you won't mind the effrontery. Just showing up on your doorstep."

"I believe it can be said I always mind effrontery."

Paul knew he was not a particularly good interviewer. His strengths as a filmmaker (if he could be said to have strengths, with only one produced film to his name), were in bringing the right people together and the framing of certain shots and sequences. But when Laurence Dunne had not responded to his letter about making a retrospective for the 1973 anniversary of the tragedy, Paul decided to take a chance and visit him. He feared his letter had not been very compelling, just some obvious points about history, the significance of the Bethnal Green report, the importance of recording the memories of the aging survivors. He'd assumed, actually, that Dunne would be eager to revisit the subject. The report was his best-known achievement, and so Paul had not anticipated having any trouble getting him to participate.

"Of course. I should have phoned."

"Probably."

Dunne looked over Paul's head and waved to someone on the street behind him. The gesture seemed designed to dismiss Paul, but Paul stood fast. He had three days' leave from his job in London and was staying at a relatively cheap B and B in Stockbridge, where Dunne lived. He told himself he had time. He also had something to tell Dunne that he hadn't put in the letter. He studied Dunne's face and decided it would be best to wait until he knew the man better. Dunne had aged well: smooth skin, thick white hair. But the eyes gave him away. They were blurry, somehow older than the rest of him.

Dunne looked back at Paul and sighed. "Where are you from?"

"Bethnal Green."

He gave Paul an old magistrate's squint. "How old are you?"

"Twenty-nine."

Dunne considered a moment. "Old enough to make tea. Come in."

Three

Ada passed Constable Henderson and kept on towards the shelter. She wanted the girls to speed up, but they were getting tired. She glanced around, more and more surprised at the number of people. The waistband of her skirt was pinching her side; her bag had slipped off her shoulder and was pulling her coat along with it. She walked faster, and the tiny bones of Emma's hand moved and cracked in hers. Emma didn't seem to mind, but Ada tried to hold her hand more loosely.

She was sure she'd once been a more patient woman. Watching her children grow thin, explaining over and over why there wasn't more to eat, why there weren't warmer clothes, that it wasn't her fault, was exacting a toll. Victory was inevitable, the government promised. Peace and plenty would return. But when? How long would they have to wait?

At the next corner Tilly bent down to tie her shoe. She hopped as she did so, trying to keep up with her mother and sister, but Ada looked back and yelled, "Come on!" At the same moment, she saw a young woman she knew back in the crowd, one of the refugees she and her friends called Mrs. W. What was she carrying? Ada could make out the pretty bag—it was the same one Mrs. W. often brought into the shop—but she also had something across her chest. When Ada had been going to the shelter more regularly, she'd noticed how well Mrs. W. managed. She was registered for a bunk, and her bundle always included a pillow and sheets and extra blankets for privacy.

Blankets! Ada had left theirs by the door when they'd argued about food. All they had now for the night were the extra jumpers. She looked back again at Mrs. W. How did she do it? How did a refugee manage the dual existence so well?

The crowd was growing tighter, and suddenly a man's elbow bumped Emma's head. He turned immediately and said "Sorry" in a Yorkshire accent, but Ada frowned and pulled Emma close. Many more people than usual were going to use the shelter tonight, she realized. Of course. She should have thought of it sooner. She was both scared about what it meant—a terrible raid; everyone sensed it—and furious with herself for not planning better. She'd told the girls she'd get a bunk. What if she couldn't?

"I'm sorry," she said.

"Mum?" Tilly asked. "Is everything all right?"

Ada looked at Tilly. Her daughter's face was not beautiful, but it combined all the best features of hers and her husband Robby's. His cheekbones, her brown eyes and pretty lips. Emma was actually the lovelier of the two, with blond hair and a set of features that seemed to be of her own invention or from generations long ago. Ada loved the two of them more than she ever said and was terrified the war wouldn't end before they were grown. She'd told no one that she was haunted by a recurring nightmare in which she hovered over her girls in their last seconds, their faces perfect, their eyes appealing to her for help, the backs of their heads crushed by something she hadn't seen.

"Yes," she said. "Of course. Just keep moving. We're almost there."

The shelter in Bethnal Green was adapted from an unfinished Tube station. It opened officially in October 1940, though the East Enders had been using it, in desperate and chaotic fashion, from the start of the war. At first the makeshift space was dark and overcrowded. Criminals and rodents plagued it. Then the government, recognizing a disaster in the making, whitewashed the walls, put in bunks, assigned wardens, and turned the station into a model unit of deep shelter. It had only one entrance, however, in the corner of the public garden at the junction of Bethnal Green and Cambridge Heath roads. The Church of St. John's stood opposite, and the superstition, left over from the early days, was to turn and look over your left shoulder at the church's blue doors before descending the shelter steps. A prayer for safety from any number of horrors.

Rev. McNeely, the young rector of St. John's, often stood on the church porch and watched the shelterers descend. He'd come to Bethnal Green from the country, a small village church, and many in the area had had their doubts, particularly as he was half-Scottish and, rumour was, homosexual. But in 1939 he'd cleared the St. John's crypt to give them a safer communal shelter, before the government even acknowledged what was happening in the Tube. They never forgot that when they needed shelter, he—a fresh young recruit from Bury St. Edmunds—had found it for them, without sermonizing on the sanctity of the space. In a neighbourhood moving away from the stringencies of faith and tired of plans and pamphlets from the government, this established him as being appealingly unorthodox.

An iron roof covered the wooden gates of the shelter entrance. Just inside, nineteen steps led down to a small landing; then a second flight of seven steps turned at a right angle into the circular booking hall. This design gave rise to the possibility, should a rush occur, of a straight line of pressure from the crowd outside to the people on the stairs. However, the most dangerous feature, according to the borough authorities, was the escalators that led from the booking hall down to the tunnels. It was here that the authorities feared a bottleneck, so shelter protocol called for wardens to man the top of the escalators at all times in order to control the flow.

The crowd moved around the knot of Constable Henderson and the boys with torches, very orderly, as always, and comfortably unconcerned. This was the population of London that had been the enemy's initial target; these were the East Enders, whom the Queen could look in the face only after Buckingham Palace was hit; these were the subjects who best understood that the war plan required courage at home. They had always done their part.

The clerk lost the green soles in the crowd. He was walking alongside Bethnal Green Gardens now, and, as the railings between pavement and park had been removed for scrap some time ago, he drifted in and found an empty bench near the pond. The siren wailed, but Bertram thought he might wait it out. Some thought the park was lucky because no bombs had ever fallen there. He assumed the German pilots understood the richer darkness of fields and trees as well as he did. The poles dotting the field, put up to deter enemy planes from landing, were more ominous to him. All the noise startled from sleep a family of ducks in the reeds at the edge of the pond. They rustled and flapped their wings as they tried again and again to settle. One of them finally broke away and headed out for a solitary paddle.

He remembered early in the war when Clare found him wandering in the street after a raid. It was only their second meeting, but she walked him home. The house next to his had been hit, and to his surprise she came in and helped him clean up all the dust and broken plaster. When everything was in order, she turned off the lights, opened the blackout curtain, and sat all night watching for planes. "It's going to be all right," she said. The chestnuts outside his window, too near the bomb, had lost all their leaves. Down the street, the trees were unharmed, thick summer foliage rustling in a breeze.

After that she found some yellow muslin, too hideous even for wartime clothes, and cut shapes from it for the inside lining of the blackout curtain. Flowers, moons, stars, and snowflakes. She began opening and closing the curtain, the daily rhythm of it a comfort: Bertram had lived with it closed for six months. She'd moved in, Bertram realized, and he was enormously glad. Now he couldn't even remember what it had felt like to sleep alone.

The following spring, willow herb, clover, and yarrow began to grow over the bomb site next door, and the makeshift meadow became the base for a thuggish family of sparrows. Clare said they must have lived in the ruined building's eaves and been too stubborn to leave. One seemed able to fly only short distances; two others lacked an eye, a tuft of loose feathers where the shiny black bead should have been. They veered and glanced around, suspicious. When Clare brushed her hair in the morning, she pulled the soft brown tangles from her brush and left them on the outside windowsill. A week ago one of the sparrows had finally used a bit in her nest.

It seemed impossible to Bertram that his feet should be the reason he was home watching sparrows instead of fighting. He'd heard of others who'd been refused for bad teeth, bad eyesight, lower-back pain. The decisions of high command were inscrutable. How could any of these conditions be grave enough to keep him at home? He'd volunteered for every bit of civil-defence training— gas, fire, rescue—and heard that his youth and strength would be valuable on the home front. When the Home Guard formed, he joined a company. In his group of twenty-five men, one had a withered arm, one was mentally deficient, one had a glass eye that fell out whenever he leaned over, and two were in the advanced and most obvious stages of venereal disease. Bertram didn't pity them; most were veterans and pitied him.

As he sat in the park, Bertram kicked his boots against the ground. It had been a long winter, and he hoped spring would come early. The next season was always anticipated—a warm summer, a crisp autumn—as if better weather would somehow ease the burden of war.

Two hours before the alert, chief shelter warden James Low reported to his post. He expected large numbers in the shelter that night and wanted to make sure everything was in order. He had four wardens on duty: Edwards, Bagshaw, Clarke, and Bryant, plus his deputy shelter warden, Hastings. He trusted them to follow their standing orders, posted on the wall in the office, but he reminded himself to check later if Clarke was in uniform. In the absence of regular enemy raids, he'd noticed his wardens growing lazy about wearing their white tin hats.

Low watched the early arrivals from his desk in the booking hall. He spoke briefly to the many he knew, nodded to the faces he recognized. The calm and methodical manner of his charges routinely impressed him. It was not hard to imagine them a population attending a concert or a festival, instead of preparing to spend the night underground during a bombing raid. He had a note from the first-aid post that they were short of one nurse, so when he saw Clare Newbury come in with her sketchbook, he asked if she would be on call.

"Of course."

A few minutes later Bill Steadman approached and asked, as he always did, whether it might be all right for him to help in the booking hall instead of descending to the shelter proper.

"Yes, Bill. We could use you tonight. Why don't you take your post at the bottom of the stairs?"

Bill clutched his chest with his left hand. "My heart thanks you." He suffered from a weak heart, supposedly, but had served often and well as an unofficial part-time warden.

Walking Bill to the stairs reminded Low that he wanted to check the bulkhead light above the stairway. If it needed to be replaced, he wanted to do it himself. He'd tried several times to persuade the local council to change the entrance, either by redesigning the approach or putting in a centre rail, but his efforts had failed. The best he could do now, he thought, was make sure there was always sufficient light. He changed the burned-out twenty-five-watt bulb. He didn't need a stool. He could easily reach it from the twelfth step down. He removed the partly blacked-out glass covering, screwed in the bulb, then adjusted it so that as far as possible the light struck the edge of the first step down. He shook his head. The stairway was still extremely dim, but for every complaint he received about the stairs being too dark, he also got one about the spill of light showing on the pavement outside.

Low had been chief warden since the Bethnal Green shelter opened. Before that he'd been an air-raid warden, volunteering as early as the summer of 1938. That autumn he'd worked almost every night with dozens of other wardens in the Bethnal Green Gardens, their exercises accompanied by loud gramophone recordings of exploding bombs, except on those nights when the lady wardens attended. Then they turned the volume down so that the bombs sounded like gentle pops, a precaution that made little sense to him or anyone else, but before the war it had felt civilized to indulge in these niceties. The enemy, they thought, didn't have such refinement.

In 1939, Low and the other early volunteers filled sandbags, put up the anti-aircraft poles, and dug trenches in the parks. They dug the trenches in straight lines, and they dug them again in zigzags for greater safety. Low learned to identify poison gas, administer first aid, call out rescue or medical services in the event of an incident, and direct people to street shelters. In one exercise he'd driven around the borough at dusk, tossing coloured tennis balls out of the window—red for gas, yellow for incendiaries, green for an unexploded bomb—instructing people on the relevant safety procedures. Most people just tossed the balls straight back, though never the refugees, he'd noted. They listened—always wide-eyed—and did not make jokes of his directions, he told his wife.

He remembered her response. "If that surprises you, you're not paying attention."

After the first rush of regular shelter users, people trickled in for a time. Then at ten past eight Low heard the deputy warden's relay wireless go off, a sure though unofficial sign of an alert. At 8:17 p.m., the sirens began.

Four

Before the boy arrived on his doorstep, Laurence Dunne had spent the morning at the club. Rushing home to catch a Wimbledon match on television, he'd swerved and hit a fox in the road, killing it instantly. Laurie was a good driver, possessing excellent hand-eye coordination and the reflexes of a sportsman. His height as a younger man had served him well, and—although he was beginning to bend towards the earth—he still stood six feet tall and could see well clear of the bonnet. That was not the problem. When he hit the fox, Laurie was craning his neck out of the side window, gauging the weather for angling—the preoccupation of his retirement—the next day. So far the weather during June 1972 had been less than satisfactory. The car rushed on, and the small reddish body spun under the hedgerow and lay still, as if sleeping.

If Laurie had known, he would have felt remorse, but he didn't much believe in apologizing.

He was mistaken about the time of the match, and so, though he parked carelessly on the gravel drive and rushed into his house on Nelson Close, he missed the first set. He sighed and eased himself into his favourite chair. The afternoon was warm and sunny, a day to be outside, but he was content at the moment to watch Ilie Nastase's unconventional tactics. Among the prospective quarterfinalists, there were no Englishmen and no Australians (for Hewitt now played as a South African). There was the wild Romanian, Nastase; Hewitt, the new South African; two Spaniards, one Czech, one Frenchman, one American, and one Russian. Many thought it was the strangest list Wimbledon had ever produced, and Laurie agreed.

But his fabled concentration was waning, something few people realized, and this, combined with the champagne his old friend the mighty William had ordered at lunch to celebrate the arrival of yet another grandchild, had Laurie asleep within minutes. His head nodded, settling finally against the glossy patch on the right wing of the chair. He saw a number of children running about; then he was angling on the Tay, his favourite Scottish river.

After a while the fish, hundreds of them, began knocking about on the rocks, and he opened his eyes to see Nastase toweling his face. When he heard the knocking again, he began to move, but with little expectation of actually making it to the door in time. They'd had servants when Armorel was alive, but she had always dealt with them. He called out that he was coming, but that, too, was futile. Gravity seemed to be working on his voice as well as his body; it had dropped into a register that was difficult to project.

His legs carried him to the front door more swiftly than he'd anticipated, but a stranger on the doorstep eroded his pleasure at arriving in time. He'd hoped for a visit from Mrs. Beckford. Bettina. She called in on him now and then, always with a little package of something as an excuse—half a dozen fresh scones, some hyacinths from the garden.

The boy on the doorstep was flustered. "Sir Laurence," he said. "I'm Paul Barber. I wrote to you about the thirtieth anniversary of the Bethnal Green report?"

Another fabled component of Laurie's reputation: putting people at ease. He'd given it up.

The boy looked intelligent and sincere, qualities Laurie required. However, points against him included ridiculous sideburns and wide lapels. Barber must have noticed him staring, because he raised a hand and smoothed one cheek. Laurie had read his letter and had simply not yet worked out how he wanted to participate in this retrospective the boy had in mind. Laurie was surprised, and not a little piqued, to be contacted by such an amateur filmmaker. Still, the boy's surname interested him, and when Laurie ran through the remainder of his day and saw that it contained nothing more exciting than an omelet for supper, he gave in.

"Where are you from?"

"Bethnal Green."

That had not been in the letter. Laurie squinted.

"How old are you?"

"Twenty-nine."

Laurie's mind did the familiar calculation: born during the war. He was taking a risk, he knew. Tragedies, when they became documentaries, usually changed. They turned fuzzy, he thought. Laurie hesitated but then opened the door wide and turned down the hall. At least the boy could make tea.

Barber stepped in quickly and asked a question Laurie ignored. Absurd to talk in this configuration. He would wait until they were seated. Laurie moved slowly, partly because he had to, and partly to give the boy behind him a chance to calm down and notice all the awards and other decorations on the wall.

Five

The woman in front of Ada lost her balance and stepped back, bringing the point of her heel down on the top of Ada's foot. Ada's eyes turned hot with tears, and she limped a few steps. Suddenly Emma flinched and leaned into her. "Watch out!" Ada yelled. Their part of the crowd flowed into the entrance, and just before the darkness of the stairs, she saw that Mrs. W. was in front of them. Ada couldn't believe it. How had she managed to get all the way up front? What if there wasn't room in the shelter for everyone tonight? Why was the crowd moving so slowly? She looked for a warden or a constable. She tried to lift Emma on to her hip, but the crowd was too tight. She took her hand and squeezed it, pulled Tilly to her other side, and started down the steps.

The clerk heard an explosion to the north. The ducks took flight, and the certainty of their decision made Bertram leave the park and head back along Cambridge Heath, towards the shelter. The road teemed with people, many of them running. This was unusual. Had the explosion unnerved them? He looked around for someone he knew. He thought he spotted Constable Henderson, but when Bertram called out, the man didn't turn. When Bertram was still quite far from the entrance to the shelter, the crowd began to slow. He was only as far as the chip shop, yet people around him were beginning to jockey for space. Yelling and shouting came from up ahead, but Bertram couldn't make out the words. He thought of the shelter, its smells and mosquitoes, and suddenly wanted to go home. Clare would find him. They'd planned to meet at their regular place—he had their blankets and the new sketchbook—but she would figure out what had happened. If the raid was bad, or if it went on all night, they could go to the building's cellar.

The shouting from up ahead grew louder for a moment, and then someone near Bertram said, "It's gone off." The suggestion coursed through the crowd, its power and path nearly visible. In the next instant, the mass quieted but turned more fierce, a single image now assembled in its mind. Bombs, a fire raid, the retaliation for what they'd done to Berlin. Bertram tried to turn, but there were so many people, he couldn't. Fear filled his chest then, like a sudden infection, a fever, turning his head hot and his bowels cold all at once. He wanted Clare. He wanted to be with her in the bunk along the curve of the tunnel. At the start of the war, he'd wondered how anyone could sleep where trains ran and people spat. Then, the hard, gritty surfaces and the nearness of strangers' bodies had revolted him. Now all that mattered was quiet. Sleep. The peace and rest of almost safety. He closed his eyes and imagined it, his body stretching along the wall, taking the cold and the damp, Clare's along his. She didn't need a lot of protecting, but this he could do.

Constable Henderson heard someone call his name, but he didn't respond. Best now to blend in, he thought. He told himself there was still time to get to his post. He'd work his way to the front and, once there, calm everyone down. But as the crowd grew closer, worry flooded in. "Wait!" he called. "Let me through!" No one paid any attention. "Let me through!"

At the bottom of the first flight of steps, Ada let go of Tilly. Just for an instant. Then she and the girls stumbled on to the landing, where they were steadied by a strong man reaching towards them in the crowd. With her right hand, Ada started Tilly down the second flight of seven steps, safely into the booking hall. Ada's left hand, arm outstretched, still held Emma. But something was happening: people were falling on to the last step above the landing, and she felt Emma's small hand slip. Ada heard her cry, "Mama!"—then she was gone. The stairwell seemed to swallow her; the weight of the falling crowd sucked her in. "My daughter's in there!" Ada screamed, and she clawed at the people in her way. A few seconds later, she turned to one person for help, a warden in a white tin hat. But when she saw the terror and confusion on this man's face, she became silent, full of purpose. She would have to get Emma out by herself. The people were jumbled together, like fingers clasped in wretched, twisting prayer. Ada ran at the mass of fallen, interlocked bodies again and again, her daughter still calling.

Bertram stretched up as tall as he could, trying to see what was keeping the crowd back. All he could see was a jostling black mass darker than the night. He smelled sweat on his shirt, and the breath and sweat of the people all around. His stomach heaved, his mouth convulsed as if it were not his own. He knew this street; it had always seemed spacious. He remembered a bus accident that had once blocked the junction for hours, but that was a crowd paralysed by tragedy. This was a crowd in motion, a crowd with a destination, unprepared to change its course. Bertram felt elbows and shoulders; tears and sweat covered his cheeks, but he couldn't raise his hands to wipe them—his arms were pinned. Nothing looked or felt right: even the branches above seemed reaching and wrong. He thought of the plans he'd had, Clare at the shelter, her slow smile when she saw the sketchbook. The crowd compressed even more—he couldn't draw a deep breath—and then Bertram, temperate and kind, who would have said compassion would last longer, struggled to get his arms up, his hands on the back of the man in front of him. The crowd pressed tighter, friend against neighbour, teacher against student, mother against child, shouting, screaming, crying.

Inside the station, Warden Low couldn't see the chaos unfolding outside, but when he looked up from his desk and saw empty space where there should have been a queue at the escalators, he was among the first to understand. If the booking hall was empty, there was an obstruction at the entrance. He immediately called the police station to report an accident, then sprinted across the booking hall. "For God's sake, keep back!" he cried. People were falling from the upper steps, one after another, already several layers deep. Bill Steadman was there, reaching and pulling, but within seconds there was a solid wall of people filling the space between the bottom step and the ceiling. The edge of the mass looked as if it should tip down on to the landing, but it did not.

Wardens Clarke and Bryant abandoned the escalators and came to help. Hastings and Edwards were already there. So was Steadman, holding a baby, tears streaming down his face. Low cried out instructions, but everyone flailed and pulled helplessly at the trapped people. A woman next to him was flying at the wall of arms and legs and shoes and heads. Low reached down and took hold of a fallen woman's arm, sure that if he could just clear her, the nearest to the landing, then the people behind would follow. There would be injuries, of course, but not a disaster. He pulled and pulled; reached up farther so that one of his hands was around her shoulder, the other on her wrist; tried to lever her out that way. He pushed at the man on top of her, trying to make room, then gave up and grabbed the arm again. Abandoning all caution, he pulled as hard as he could. Nothing! He fell back, the arm slipping from his grasp, and he saw that it was lifeless.

Six

Dunne sat at the table and talked about tennis while Paul fumbled with the pot and water. Now and then Dunne offered a direction or a location, and Paul slowly assembled the tray: cups, saucers, sugar, milk. He'd read up on angling, had even brought a fly in his bag should the conversation go that way, but today fish seemed to be the furthest thing from Dunne's mind. On and on he went, about the new rackets, the new training, the new physique. Nastase's cunning; Stan Smith's decorum. In the quarter-finals the American had impressed Dunne, it was clear, but Paul had to work hard to stay focused on what Dunne was saying about it. When they moved to the living room, Paul noticed the house was grand but overstuffed, decorated not quite as the country retreat he'd expected. Instead it felt like a room holding the furniture and memorabilia of a life lived a long time ago somewhere else. Paul glanced out of the window and hoped for rain; then the television might be turned off and Dunne would talk about something other than tennis.

When he looked back, Dunne was staring at him and Paul suspected he'd missed something.

"It's an excellent tournament," Dunne said. "But maybe you don't like sport."

Remembering what he'd read, Paul made a quick calculation. In his prime, the man before him had been known for his intelligence, his wit, his empathy across classes. As a magistrate before the war, he'd presided with a total disregard for public opinion, which, in Dunne's view, was usually wrong. He was a man people trusted—lawyers, police officers, officials of his court. Even, it was said, the criminals who appeared before him.

"I'm sorry, sir. My concern today is so far from that world that I'm a bit distracted."

"Yes, the report. Well, I could remind you that wars are won and lost on the playing fields of Eton. Perhaps I won't."

Paul tried to be jovial. "But you just did."

Dunne laughed. "Indeed!"

Paul thought they were making progress, but then Dunne drained his tea, made a face, and looked at him. "What is it you think you want to know?"

Paul braced himself around his teacup. He could be straightforward and say that at the moment he simply wanted to know if Dunne would agree to an on-camera interview for the documentary. Or he could begin a conversation about the significance of the Bethnal Green report in 1943. Undecided, he nearly revealed too much too soon.

"I was . . . a child in Bethnal Green."

Dunne frowned. "You've told me."

"And so I've wondered how you managed such a thorough investigation in such a short time."

Dunne was still frowning when Paul said, "How did you write the report?"

Dunne released the frown, and slumped in his chair. "It was very difficult. How do you think I did it?"

Paul looked down, and when he looked up, his expression had changed. This was one of his better tactics. "You remind me of my father, Sir Laurence," he said. "I don't think he ever answered a question without asking one. 'How do you catch a trout, Dad?' 'What do you suggest, Paul?' It pushed me, of course."

What he was saying was a lie. Growing up, he hardly ever saw his father, but the story was a way to introduce angling, which

Paul hoped would help him succeed with Dunne. To keep his bearings, he pressed his right heel hard into the floor while he spoke, a habit that had replaced the nervous bounce that plagued him when he was younger.

Dunne squinted at him.

Paul changed course. "You were a relatively unknown magistrate—"

"Not true."

"You were the youngest Bow Street magistrate, but you were popular."

Dunne nodded.

"And because of that, a defensive government obsessed with morale asked you to go into a close-knit community grieving over a terrible accident. Somehow in three weeks' time, you produced a report that became a model of style and substance."

Dunne held up a hand to stop him. "Your father was an angler?"

The muscles of Paul's right leg began to burn.

"Yes. In fact, I'd hoped to show you something." He reached into the bag by his feet and pulled out a fly wrapped in a piece of tissue paper. "He tried to teach me, but, well, I wish I'd paid more attention." He held out the small trout fly, a pale evening dun. He fancied the name.

"What do you think?"

Copying from a book, Paul had tied it himself with some wool and a feather. The result was mediocre at best, and he knew it was a risk. Dunne, the master angler, would either see through the lie or be intrigued by the effort.

Paul held his breath when Dunne hesitated. Then the magistrate squinted and took it.

Seven

For hours the borough bellowed. Sirens arrived, departed, returned. The nearly one thousand people already inside the shelter awaited word, filtered rumours: there was an unexploded bomb, a woman had dropped her baby, an enemy plane had crashed. The most persistent rumour: the entrance had taken a direct hit. This had happened most recently at Bank, where fifty-six people had been killed. But in the odd currency of war, the evaluating and calibrating that went into surviving, fifty-six felt lucky. Everyone wondered how many would be dead tonight.

Listening to the unruliness above, everyone inside began to hush. How easy when you were safe! Two nurses took care of them, while all other rescue workers tried to quell the misery at the entrance. People arranged blankets; families settled down.

Outside, constables ran about, tapping people with their batons, pushing and pulling, trying to move people away from the stairs. Not until the all-clear sounded and the pressure from the top of the steps finally eased could any sense be made of the scene. The bodies of the few still alive and the many dead formed a tangled mass of such complexity that the work of extrication was interminably slow. Warden Low lifted the last casualty from the stairway just before midnight. He put Emma Barber on a stretcher himself.

After a roll call of the shelter's registered users, Low told his staff to go home. The roll call had been the idea of Hastings, the deputy warden, and it might have been better to have cancelled it. Silence followed the calling of name after name.

"Go home," Low said. He wanted to say more. He thought he should try to organize them, remind them of their responsibilities, because with work came order and with order, hope. But sending his staff home seemed the only just and reasonable thing to do. They were dishevelled and demoralized beyond sense. He thought he and the nurses could look after the shelterers already in for the night.

"There'll be a public inquiry in the morning," he added. "I'm sure the prime minister will call for it himself."

When everyone had dispersed, Clare Newbury told him he didn't look well.

"Where's Bertram?" he asked. He knew Clare took care of Bertram, and he was glad of it. He worried the boy would not make it through the war.

"Fine. Shaken, but fine. I sent him home, and now I'm going to ask you to sit." She moved him towards a chair near the escalators. "You will not serve this shelter by collapsing," she said kindly. He wondered why she didn't take him to his desk, but when he looked over, he saw Constable Henderson, still in uniform, slumped there.

Clare gave him a cursory examination. His pulse and blood pressure were fine; his temperature was up a bit.

"Warden Low," she said, though he heard her voice as if from a great distance, "you have a fever. It's not high, but I suggest you go home. The deputy warden can finish the night."

This was correct procedure, but he'd never left his post early. He looked around the hall. In the yellow light of several dim bulbs, the cement floor and walls of the shelter looked damp, sickly, feverish, themselves. Bill Steadman, his unofficial warden, was sitting on the floor, shaking his head so slowly, Low thought that he must be asleep. Then he realized the man was wide-awake. Several wardens brought up a few of the curious from the platforms below. There wasn't much to see—all the dead were gone. There were just the seven dirty stairs leading up to the landing. These were blocked by police barriers, so the group huddled to the right to peer up the first nineteen steps. Not much to see there, either. Just more concrete stairs, with a wooden edge to the treads soaked with fluids he didn't want to think about.

"Where is Hastings?"

"Outside. The police are taking statements."

He nodded. "Check on Steadman there, will you? I'm afraid he's in some kind of shock."

"Not much remedy for it," she said, "but I'll see what I can do."

He thanked her, then picked up his coat and squeezed past the police barriers. In a few hours the shelterers would have to leave by the emergency exit half a mile down the tunnel, but he hugged the right-hand wall of the stairwell and stepped quickly, leaving the shelter the way so many thousands had come and gone safely before that night. At the top he skirted a second set of police barriers and joined the disorganized crowd. No one saw him, or he was sure he'd have been asked for a statement. There was Hastings, talking to a constable. He started walking but stopped in front of St. John's. He almost shook his fist at the cross, dark against the sky, but it was a gesture too full of defiance for the defeat he felt. Instead he sat on a step. He thought about going back—he would put something right before morning—but he knew it would be impossible to look at the staircase again. Just the thought of it made him gag. He stood, stumbled, and nearly fell. Then he shoved his fists in his pockets and aimed for home.

Later the events of 3 March, 1943 would be examined and re-examined, but mainly regretted for innumerable reasons, yet one stood out above all: not a single bomb had fallen on the city that night.

Eight

Laurie thought the would-be filmmaker had been sitting strangely. Did he need to use the lavatory? All through the interview it had looked to Laurie as if the boy were about to spring out of the chair. What was this? Some new, ill-fitting garment that didn't allow one comfort in sitting? But when Barber stood to leave, Laurie looked at his trousers and thought them fine, if a bit worn.

It certainly was odd to have been contacted by someone named Barber, though it was clear he couldn't be from the family Laurie remembered. His skin was too dark. Laurie had talked to him for the better part of the afternoon, even though it was clear that the boy knew very little about angling. Laurie had neither agreed nor refused to participate in the film project. He told Barber he needed time to think, and that's what he was doing. He always thought best on a riverbank.

The Test was overstocked this year, and, despite the good weather, Laurie wasn't enjoying the day. He wanted to be in Scotland, angling alone. Instead he had various club members all around: Clarkson on the opposite bank, Vane some way down; and a minute earlier, Smith and Headley had trudged past, heading to a beat upstream, where Smith would no doubt stir up the silt and weeds by wading, a regular habit of his, although it was against the river rules.

People can move on land and through air and even reach the depths of the ocean, Laurie marvelled. What they can't do—

inhibited by nature and temperament—is find a good lie and stay there. Though he'd tried, God knows.

A minute later, Laurie's line went taut, and after a good race upstream and down, he had a fifteen-inch rainbow in the shallows. While he was reeling it in, a second, larger rainbow nipped at the fly. He looked towards the clubhouse with disgust. "Why don't we just scoop them out with nets?" he said aloud.

On the opposite bank, Clarkson turned, but Laurie lowered his head over the fish. He would speak to Mortimer, the river keeper, at lunch.

As he cast again, he reflected on the history he'd studied, a sort of general sweep. Egypt, Rome, the roiling Dark Ages. The Renaissance, of course, then the Industrial Revolution, and the wars. He saw paintings and shadows and costumes; himself, too, in the libraries of Eton and Magdalen, studying the books that had informed him of these things. The review lasted a minute or two, time enough for him to score another trout and cast again, and afterwards he decided crowded places were a nuisance.

He rubbed a hand across his eyes. He was thinking of crowds because of Barber. He might have been happy never to have discussed them again, until the boy showed up on his doorstep. Was that true? He couldn't be sure. He was aware of an eagerness seeping in, a desire to talk about the incident that made him uncomfortable.

He started back to the clubhouse. Crowds, as far as he could tell, had rarely done any good. Where they did succeed, and perhaps the rural riots in Wales were an example, they offered only temporary support for a dying way of life. Crowds were blinded by their credulity, he thought, their exaggeration of good and evil. Yes. He would propose the idea later and hoped the subject might just make his friend mighty William forget his bloody grandchildren for one afternoon.

Lunch was salmon with hollandaise sauce, and the group ate

outside under a white tent on the lawn. Most of the older members disliked eating outside, but the younger ones insisted on it, so this season the club's twenty-four members had voted to hold several of these "garden lunches" as an experiment. Laurie did not oppose eating outside, but he found several of the younger members insufferable in their determination. Why join a club and then immediately try to change it? For nearly one hundred and fifty years, the members had eaten in the oak-panelled grill room, the sun reduced to liquid through its lead glass windows. He had a dozen memories for every table: he'd dined in the corner with Andrew when he'd come down from Oxford; he'd celebrated there with friends when he became chief metropolitan magistrate; the whole place had been filled for his retirement party. He knew what the room felt like dressed for morning tea and how it behaved when cigar smoke hung in folds from the rafters at midnight.

Now the club owned a bright white tent with poles of questionable strength. It came from an American company, and the staff were still assembling various parts when the salad course arrived. Lanyards thrashed about in the wind, putting Laurie in mind of the coast, and a piece of the tent at Laurie's end—a door-shaped bit with clear plastic parts that were meant to suggest windows, he feared—flapped about like a leeward sail. The younger members looked worried, their experiment failing, while many of the older members were too busy trying to align their white folding chairs on the uneven grass or dodging bees to notice much of anything.

Laurie turned to mighty William, engaged in spearing a tomato. "Crowds, Will. I don't like them."

William looked up, his fork in mid-air. He glanced around the tent, shook his head briefly at the staff's effort with the ropes in the far corner. "Crowds? Surely it isn't crowded today. Hamilton and Warren aren't even here."

"In a general sense. Demonstrations and such."

William looked blank.

"Any crowd-driven idea. Human slavery! Tulip mania! The war!"

"Oh, no. I suppose not." William rested his fork on the edge of the plate. "What made you think of it?"

"The river today."

"Overstocked."

"Certainly. Did you mention it to the river keeper?"

"I thought you had."

Laurie could not remember if he had or not. "I will," he said quickly, confidently.

"Good."

Laurie studied William. He couldn't believe how old he looked, but then William would probably have said the same thing about him. He could recall William as a younger man, famous for his wit, throwing comments at a conversation like a hunter throwing spears. Laurie couldn't remember where the "mighty" joke had come from, if it had had to do with banking, conversation, or angling. Maybe all of them. Suddenly he thought he might ask William what to do about the boy's documentary; he would probably understand the problems. Laurie reached for his water, but his hand shook, and the glass, perspiring in the June heat, slipped out of his hand. The mighty William righted it before anyone else at the table noticed.

Grateful, Laurie smiled. "How are the grandchildren?" he asked.

Drying his hands with Laurie's napkin—the settings were all askew—William beamed. "Oh, the devils!" They were coming to visit, all five of them, and he had no idea where he was going to put them.

Nine

The next morning, Bethnal Green woke to a quiet dawn, a city going about its business, geese flying overhead, the fire department pigs snuffling as they moved to their pen in the Museum Gardens. A cold front had come in behind the warmer air and sent all hope of an early spring skittering away like the petals and feathers in the gutters. There were no angry mobs or fiery newspaper headlines. No outraged prime minister calling for an inquiry, no monarch full of compassion and remorse. The king was on a short holiday in Northumberland, actually, due back on a train some time on Saturday. The only evidence of the tragedy was the presence of two constables posted by the entrance to the shelter and the battered police barriers they stood behind. There was not even a list of the dead posted, as usually followed a raid.

Overnight, some authority had made a decision: the accident would be kept secret. The large number of dead was difficult to hide, however, so after a few hours the authorities announced that the shelter had, in fact, taken a small, direct hit. The population of Bethnal Green, puzzled by the total absence of any bomb damage, remained unconvinced. Then it began to rain, the perfect climate for rumour: it was Fascist incitement, a Jewish panic, an Irishman holding the gate against the crowd. There'd been a land mine, a new German weapon, a gas leak.

In the afternoon a crowd gathered at St. John's. The people were hesitant about enquiring after friends and relatives but could not resist gathering where chance might deliver the news. Many were nervous and helpful while they waited but then collapsed or dissolved in fury when they learned the one they'd hoped for was dead. Some wandered inside the church to the pews, and some sat in the drizzle on the front steps, the temperature difference between the two not significant enough to inspire religious devotion in those not already so inclined. Rev. McNeely worked tirelessly, silently, bringing blankets and handkerchiefs to those inside and out. He was sleepless and pale, poorly clothed and obviously cold, but he moved with such conviction, no one thought to slow him down.

Ada sat on a corner of the porch, wrapped in a brown coat, rocking. Her chin-length hair was ragged from rain. There was a raw spot on each palm where she'd dug in her nails when they pulled her away from the stairs. She kept thinking about Emma's birth. Wasn't that a severing followed by a reunion? This had been a severing, so wouldn't Emma be returned to her? Birth, death, reunion—the ideas grew confused in her mind.

She knew she should go home. She kept thinking she had, so well could she picture the walk up the road to their house. Over and over again she thought she'd got up and was walking— she could feel just how to do it—but then she'd look down and discover her legs were still bent, her hands wrapped around her ankles, her cheeks pressed into her knees.

"There was room along the right for an instant," she said, then waited for the church bells to finish chiming the half hour before continuing. "That's how Tilly and I, and I thought . . ."

"Hush," the women nearest her said. "Hush." They patted and petted her.

In the streets around the church few people spoke. Those who did shook their heads and whispered. Approaching and offering help seemed too loud an action in the borough-wide stillness. The mourners on the church steps were not the usual bombed-out homeless; they were not the disconnected victims of indifferent bombs. An awkward feeling grew: these mourners had survived a tragedy in which they'd somehow played a role, and no one knew what to do.

Every now and then someone pointed at the shelter entrance, then up the road, tracing lines of approach, recounting what had happened. It was said that an off-duty constable had hoisted himself over the fallen people and in this way climbed from the top to the bottom of the accident but was still unable to do any good. Someone else said they'd heard about a woman who arrived late. She'd got in, but over ground she thought unusually soft. Later she knew she must have walked on bodies.

The people stared, listening to the same stories again and again. They shook their heads. The impossible idea: the victims (no one knew how many—some said one hundred, others five hundred) had died for nothing. There had been no bombs.

Without anyone asking him to, before anyone had any idea of the nature and extent of the accident at Bethnal Green, while the crew organized by the Regional Commissioners in the early morning hours after the disaster was still sweeping and scrubbing the steps, Warden Low resigned from his position at the shelter. He simply wrote a letter and posted it to the home secretary, Herbert S. Morrison. Warden Low would have written to the king if he'd known how. Then he sat in his kitchen and waited for dawn, for Sarah, for her help once again in making sense of the world.

How would he tell her? They'd never had children, never conceived. This was the great disappointment of her life. Early in the war, they'd heard a baby crying in a collapsed building, and she'd dug among the broken cement for hours until she found the boy, alive.

Low felt Sarah's hand on his shoulder. He opened his eyes. "James?" she said. "What's wrong?"

"I thought we needed more light and that it would be all right." He gulped from his mug, but the coffee he'd made and poured for them was cold.

"What would be all right? James, what's happened?"

"It rained," he started. "The stairs were slippery." When he didn't continue, Sarah pressed a hairclip into the back of her up-swept grey hair and put the coffee away. Tea and coffee each had a place: tea for comfort, coffee for courage. But what James needed now, she thought, was brandy. She opened the cabinet beneath the sink.

"Sarah," James said, so quietly she barely heard him. "Something terrible's happened."

Sarah didn't turn. "I know, and you're going to tell me. But wait a minute while I get us settled."

She set out the brandy, two small glasses, and started peeling the potatoes for breakfast. Serve potatoes for breakfast three times a week, the Potato Plan advised. Lord help us, Sarah thought. She switched on the wireless so that their neighbours wouldn't be able to hear whatever it was James had to say. She'd been married to him for thirty-five years, and if he'd done something wrong at the shelter, he was still the best man she knew.

While she was moving about the kitchen, he began to tell her that he'd replaced the bulb above the stairs in the shelter, the one in the ceiling above the first flight down. It was the first item he'd taken care of after checking in. But he'd replaced the standard twenty-five-watt bulb with a higher-wattage bulb.

"That shouldn't matter, should it?"

"They smashed it, but I knew we needed more light." He shook his head.

"Why would they smash it?"

Low made a sound of disgust in his throat. "They worry about the bit of spill up on the pavement, that it will be seen in the blackout. It terrifies them."

"How do they do it—smash the light? With their hands?"

"I don't know. It's happened five times, at least. We've replaced the glass covering five times."

She tied her robe closed, then moved her chair around the corner of the table and pulled his glasses off.

"You're tired," she said.

"Yes." His eyes, unshielded, were watery and large.

"I bet they'll say the bulb was burned out," James said. "It was the night before, but I replaced it. First thing." Then he repeated what he'd already said about the rain, the slippery steps. Sarah pushed the brandy closer. He sipped, then mentioned his desk at the shelter, how fond of it he was, how its sturdy Victorian legs, so incongruous in the modern, straight-edged station, pleased him. They seemed a reminder of all they were fighting for.

"James," Sarah interrupted. "Please. There's enough of that on the BBC. Tell me what happened."

Her husband blanched a shade whiter and told her about the crush. Afterwards they sat in silence, holding hands, Sarah wondering about the dead, who they were; James, how death had come to them.

"You know," he started after a time. "Some of the people trapped on the stairs yelled at us to put our light out even while we were trying to help them." He swallowed and shook his head.

"Let me see your resignation."

"You can't, Sarah. It's done, sent."

"What will you do?"

He nodded, expecting the question. "I'm a fire watcher," he said. "I imagine they'll still have me."

"There are the allotments on Russia Lane," Sarah said. "You could do good work there with all you know about gardening."

"Yes," James agreed.

"The light couldn't have been the only problem."

"I'm sure it wasn't," he said.

"If they smashed it, there will be glass on the stairs. They'll see that it wasn't your fault."

James stared.

"It wasn't your fault. James?"

He hit the table with his fist. "Quiet!" His sudden anger surprised them both. When Sarah stood, she made a pot of coffee.

At the town hall Bertram was given the job of documenting the dead, recording what was in their pockets, and returning the items to the families. The mayor and deputy mayor, senior clerks and wardens—even some of the more capable members of the Home Guard—were all preoccupied with petitions from the borough council, the Regional Commissioners, the London City Council, the Ministry of Civil Defence, and the Ministry of Information. Even the Ministry of Food was concerned, about the victory gardens and window boxes that might now lie fallow if the number of dead proved to be as high as was thought. A campaign to sustain the gardening effort was suggested, with "Save the Green in Bethnal Green" proposed as a motto. Mr. Wycomb, senior clerk—a friendly man who blinked and swallowed frequently, sending his Adam's apple up and down—guffawed.

"Someone's got us confused with the West End, mate," he said.

There were also the editors and reporters, borough engineers, city engineers—all concerned with matters more critical than the contents of pockets. What had gone wrong? What could be done to prevent it from happening again? Would there be a public or a private inquiry? These questions were compelling because still unclear.

The dead, however, were clear enough. They needed to be counted and identified, their personal items returned. Mr. Wycomb put his hand on Bertram's shoulder and handed him a notebook.

Bertram's expression must have worried him. "Whatever you want, Bert. It isn't going to be easy."

"Where are they?"

"All over, I'm afraid. You might start at the hospital. Best I can tell, some are there and some are at the morgue. The maternity ward got a few of the women and children, apparently."

"And Regional Commissioners want to know what's in their pockets?"

"That's right. And bags and purses. You know. Whatever they were carrying."

"Why?"

"Not sure, mate."

"But what do they expect to find?"

Wycomb rubbed his eyes. "Who knows."

Bertram took the notebook. "Do I have to use this?" The cover was green, reminding him of the girl's shoes that night. That the job had fallen to him seemed preordained.

"Of course not. I was just trying to get you started. Do whatever you like. Maybe they want incriminating evidence. Maybe it's an assignment from those eavesdroppers, Ministry of Information. Maybe they just want to return the belongings to the families, 'who have already lost so much'"—he parodied Herbert Morrison. "I'm sure that's what we'll read in the papers. Can Clare go with you?"

"I might see."

"I would."

But when Bertram asked the next morning, Clare said she couldn't. She had an assignment from Mass Observation, for whom she volunteered.

"They're sending me into Stepney. They want to know what the Jews are saying about the accident." She was making him breakfast, and when she saw his face, she helped him gather what he'd need and pack his bag. She even walked with him part of the way to the hospital. "Are you all right?" she asked.

He nodded, but they both knew it was a lie.

"Bring everything home tonight, and I'll help you sort through it."

He nodded. "I don't think I can do this."

She kissed his forehead. "I'll help you tonight."

Alone, Clare's kiss drying on his skin, Bertram could think of nothing but the accident, how he'd been sitting in the park, watching the poplar leaves across the water. Then what? He couldn't recall, exactly. Did he walk or run? Speak or scream? He did remember the feeling of his hands on someone's back, someone else's hands on him. He'd heard a siren, a child's cry, everything enfeebled by the wind that came up suddenly around them. A shop awning flapped white above the crowd. He remembered thinking that he'd never seen so many people on the Roman Road, all converging on the shelter, streaming out of shops, climbing out of buses. The night was clear—he remembered that—but the pavement damp, amplifying the slap and grind of so many people rushing. The crowd had grown thick fast. The faces Bertram remembered were confused but not frightened. Most people were moving quickly, not talking, he thought, except for one man deep in his pints, belting out the national anthem as he ran.

And when was that? How close had Bertram been to the entrance then?

In front of the hospital gates, Bertram could smell a coal fire and damp earth, two seasons in the air on the same day. A gentle rain fell over the street, the raindrops steady enough to set the leaves all around to nodding. He tried to see it as encouragement, but it looked more like shock. He adjusted his umbrella, then crossed the street to the café next to the boarded-up Red Lion.

The shopkeeper asked how he was feeling; did he need a roll with his tea?

He shook his head.

"Are you sure? I've some left over from yesterday."

He took the roll—it seemed easier than refusing again—then

sat by the curtained window and watched the street through the large holes of cheap lace. He saw a boy of eight or nine walking with his mother. They were making slow progress, and it wasn't until they were closer that Bertram realized it was because the boy's eyes were closed. He seemed to be trying to impress his mother with his intimate knowledge of the street, naming every place as they passed with his eyes tightly closed. In front of the bombed sites, he would throw his arms up and make noises with his mouth. She remained unperturbed. Bertram saw her pause only once, when she pulled her hand out of the boy's to brush something from her cheek. Her boy's eyes popped open then, and he waited.

Tea and roll were indistinguishable (both tasted vaguely of potatoes), but Bertram began to feel better with something in his stomach. When he left, the shopkeeper called after him. "There now. I thought you were hungry!"

People want to take care of each other, he thought. Until they can't.

And when had that been? How close was he to the entrance then? His fear, what he didn't want to tell Clare, was that he might have been pushing on a dead man. How could he know? Where had the boundary been?

Ten

Paul sat a long time over breakfast. After the previous day's frustration with Dunne, he'd stayed out at the pub too late, had had too much to drink, and now all he wanted was a large glass of orange juice. Mrs. Loudon, however, seemed determined to dispense the fluid in thimblefuls. He'd already asked for three refills of the tiny juice glass, and each time she was decidedly less friendly. "Good, isn't it?" had become "Precious liquid" and finally, just this last time, "Doesn't grow on trees, does it?" To Paul she was typical of a woman of her generation, of someone who had lived through rationing, and he felt a true respect for her. He was just very thirsty. How much could orange juice cost?

He was not optimistic about his chances with Dunne. He'd found him frailer than he'd expected and vague in his interest in participating. Paul had watched the way he moved his fingers against his thigh and wondered if Dunne was aware of the tic. It had come and gone all through the afternoon while he lectured on tennis and reminisced about the war. Interview subjects needed a chance to warm up, Paul knew, and good material might eventually come. But he worried about how much time this might take.

In the corner, an American couple finished their cereal and leaned over their guidebooks. The placement of the tables in Mrs. Loudon's small breakfast nook forced Paul to face the only other occupant, a gentleman eating alone. They both assiduously avoided eye contact.

Suddenly Mrs. Loudon came swinging through the kitchen

door, sloshing a large jug of water. She set it down next to Paul's plate, then banged out again.

It seemed like a good sign. He'd got her to concede that she owned larger vessels! If he could do that, he could get Dunne, he hoped. Imagining just how he might tell Dunne what he hadn't put in his letter, he began to smile.

Eleven

Without Emma, Tilly spent most of her time alone. Her mother had gone to bed; her father was running the greengrocer's. Tilly's only jobs were to attend school, when it was open, and run errands on the way home.

Since the accident she'd seen reporters in the area—everyone had—but the teachers told the children not to talk to them. Then one afternoon Tilly saw a reporter with sweets. He was talking to a group of her older schoolmates in the park. The girls had short, swingy coats, warmer than Tilly's. The boys were serious, shaking their heads. Tilly couldn't see if anyone took the sweets or not.

She sat down on a bench and slouched considerably so that her feet would not dangle. She wanted them solidly on the ground. When the older children walked away, the reporter saw Tilly, and she let him approach. If he knelt or patted her head, she decided, she would leave. If he stood and talked properly, she would listen.

As it happened, the reporter stood, and the sweet he had left was liquorice. Emma loved liquorice. But when Tilly remembered she couldn't share it with Emma, she held her breath and tried to leave. Then the reporter made another offer, a surprising offer, and Tilly was intrigued by the idea that something she could say had that much value. So she told him about the stairwell, the large number of dead people she'd seen, the woman who had fallen first; but when he asked if she knew what had started it, she hesitated, then shook her head.

He asked if she'd seen a lot of four-by-twos.

"What?"

"Jews."

"Oh." She realized it was the rhyming slang she'd heard on the street and read on walls. She hadn't known what it meant. "I don't think so."

He asked if he could use her name. She shook her head. Could he at least say how old she was?

"Yes, that's important," Tilly agreed. "Eight." Then she stuffed the money he gave her, more than she'd expected, deep into her pocket and walked home. Her mother was asleep, but Tilly pulled out the notes and laid them on her mother's pillow one by one.

The *Times* broke the story the next day: LONDON SHELTER DISASTER, HUNDREDS CRUSHED TO DEATH, WOMAN FALLS ON STAIRS. Inspired by his source (*an eight-year-old girl who wished to remain anonymous*), the reporter went on to compare the tragedy to the disaster at Victoria Hall on 16 June 1883, when one hundred and eighty-three children were crushed to death in a doorway while rushing down from a gallery to obtain toys from Fay, a popular conjurer of the day.

The story humiliated the war-hardened workers of the East End. After all they'd endured, how could they be compared with children running after toys? A hurried, private inquiry by Ernest Gowers, one of the Regional Commissioners, did nothing to help. In a matter of hours, he concluded the incident was the result of a mass panic, case closed. The funerals began, all listed in the *East End Observer*, more than a dozen each day:

Kay Johnson, 25, seamstress, killed in disaster
Betsy Johnson, 5, daughter, killed in disaster
John Kater, 14, mason's apprentice, killed in disaster
Ruby Drake, 24, mother, killed in disaster
Sarah Drake, 2, Paul Drake, 4, killed in disaster

On and on, many more women and children than men.

A few days later Dr. Hawkesworth, coroner of Bethnal Green, revealed to the *Daily Herald* a disturbing detail: death was in all cases caused by asphyxiation. There was only one broken bone, a child's fibula. "I did not see a single case of fractured ribs," he said, "which is extraordinary, given the circumstances."

This, followed by a mealy-mouthed statement from the home secretary—"The appropriate authorities will probe, appropriately, the matter to the utmost"—stoked the tension in Bethnal Green. The East Enders knew what death looked like. Three years of aerial bombardment—the spectre of firestorms, collapsed buildings, charred and crushed bodies—had made everyone a coroner, and this quiet compression at Bethnal Green, in which some died and others lived, was, frankly, hard to believe. A gathering of mourners at St. John's gave up on stoic endurance, which had not earned them much, and marched on the police station. They demanded a public inquiry. The officers watched from the windows until one of the protesters put his foot through a car window. (In general, the people found it difficult to wreck things themselves when the enemy had succeeded so well.) That afternoon Home Secretary Morrison made a concession: the disaster would be classified as an official war accident, and reparations for survivors and victims' families would not only be granted but expedited.

Bethnal Green was mulling this over when it was discovered that the local council had sent a request to Mr. Ernest Gowers of the Regional Commissioners two years ago for alterations to the shelter entrance. The plan and correspondence, sent by Bertram Lodge, discussed the possibility of just the sort of deadly crush that had occurred.

The request had been ignored, then denied.

When this story broke, there was another mass demonstration for a public inquiry. A house-to-house petition was begun, starting with the bereaved families. The afternoon papers suggested a cover-up, evening demonstrations followed, and the next morning Morrison announced in the Commons that his initial request for an independent inquiry—what he had wanted all along, he claimed— had been granted. He'd already communicated with the popular metropolitan magistrate from Victoria Park, Laurence Dunne.

The MP from Ayrshire asked a question. "If it is found that the rumours are correct and certain persons did shout that they saw bombs falling and encouraged a stampede, will Laurie be given sufficient power to deal with the scoundrels?"

"Yes. Certainly—" Morrison began.

The MP from Maidenhead interrupted. "And if it is a cause of the rising Jewish problem? It is not clear how many more refugees—"

A mixture of shouts and cheers drowned him out.

"Let us be reasonable and trust to arithmetic rather than wild hearsay or propaganda," the MP from Ayrshire called out again. "The number of Jews in England is less than one per cent of the total population. The Jewish problem is a myth. We do not have too many!"

Morrison raised his voice over the eruption. "Let us see what the inquiry finds! Let us wait and see!" Grunts and hmms and other rumbles filled the chamber.

Twelve

Magistrate Laurence Dunne was at home at No. 17 Bonner Road, Victoria Park, London, when he received the request from the home secretary to open an inquiry. The day was 10 March 1943, Ash Wednesday, and many years later Laurie would say that he was glad of the season. With ashes on his forehead, holding Morrison's note, he felt doubly marked: for Lent and for history. All of London seemed to be watching and waiting, trying to prepare for something better.

No. 17 Bonner Road stood in a line of three-storey houses built as a terrace behind the original manor, Bethnal House, in 1700. In the eighteenth century all had become private homes, and it was this character they retained. Laurie loved Bethnal Green, its noisy community spirit, the children playing in the streets, the adults sitting outside with their tea or carrying a pint from the corner pub in a jug, but he was glad that Bonner Road was quieter. Chestnuts lined both sides of the street, and the front doors stood back from the pavement. The windows were large, two on the ground floor, three on the first, with dormers in the roof, all rarely, if ever, opened. The life of these houses faced not the street but the gardens at the back. The residents of Bonner Road all had gardens for entertaining, and when you were in them, it was almost possible to forget you were in London. Living on Bonner Road allowed Laurie to be near the area he served as magistrate yet maintain the life to which he was accustomed.

His wife, Armorel, searched his face as he read. "What's wrong?" she asked.

"That accident. I'm to investigate."

"Good," she said, putting down her sewing.

He looked at her.

"Oh, it is good," she said. "Those poor people. We need to know what happened."

Laurie shook his head, but he knew it was true. The accident had shaken the city. How could so many people—it looked like the final count would be nearly two hundred—die on a night when there wasn't even a raid? The most cursory review would have shown that the people of Bethnal Green were accustomed to heavy anti-aircraft fire and bombing. During the worst period of the bombing, absorbing wave after wave of refugees, they amazed the authorities with their exemplary behaviour. This was the home of the Bevin Boys, youths who, when selected by ballot for the mines rather than military service, protested and begged to be sent to the front. The request was refused, but all the papers celebrated the Bethnal Green spirit.

Why would they panic now? And yet that's what the Gowers inquiry, in what amounted to no more than a meeting (two hours, five witnesses), concluded. The borough deserved an investigation, Laurie agreed, a proper one. After all the bombs and fires, it was wrong to tell Bethnal Green it had lost its nerve. There had to be another cause.

The government, Morrison's note said, regretted becoming involved.

Without in any way assuming negligence in any quarter, he'd written, *we'd like you to assure us, and the public, that any avoidable defect, either in the structure and equipment of the shelter, or in the arrangements for its staffing or supervision of those within the shelter, is brought to light so that steps can be taken to minimize the risk of any repetition of this tragedy.*

Morrison went on: he was confident that Laurie—as a magistrate with a populist reputation and a home near the neighbourhood in question—would do a good job. But as far as possible, the inquiry was to be conducted in secret. *In conclusion, your inquiry must be thorough and speedy and the results candid and convincing.*

After dinner Laurie and Armorel sat in the upstairs drawing room.

"You're upset," Armorel said.

"Yes."

"Is there anything I can do?"

He shook his head.

"Have you read about the infants?"

"Yes." Somehow seven infants had survived. All were orphaned, and the papers had christened them the "shelter orphans".

Laurie raised his book, *Fly-Tying for Salmon: The Whole Art of Tying Salmon-Flies with Details of the Principal Dressings* by Eric Taverner, a signal that he wanted to be left alone. It was a compilation, bound in blue leather, of the best chapters from Mr. Taverner's monumental volume, *Salmon Fishing,* in the Lonsdale Library, with reproductions of the colour plates in that work. Armorel had given it to him for Christmas.

While he pretended to read, he thought about the task before him. His own activity on the night of 3 March was beyond reproach yet somehow humiliating. He'd had a bath, a long one, not something he did often. But that evening, after a contentious case before the court, and a potato dinner with Armorel, he'd felt worn out and sick. He'd retired to the second floor and had had a long soak. Afterwards he'd joined Armorel in the drawing room. When the alert sounded, they decided to use the Morrison shelter, the steel coffee table to which the home secretary had given his name, if they heard any bombs. Armorel moved her sewing away from the windows and Laurie took his book over to the sofa and their evening carried on. After a while they went to bed. Laurie recalled hearing the all-clear just before he fell sleep.

Why did Morrison want him to lead the inquiry? His ease with the working classes, he suspected. He'd always enjoyed popularity with a range of people. It was one reason he'd left the bar in 1936 to become a magistrate. He wanted to interpret the laws of the land first-hand, and the East End was the place to do it.

But Bethnal Green? asked his baffled family and friends. An area known for its madhouses?

They referred to two notorious asylums of the eighteenth and nineteenth centuries, the White House and the Red House. In 1920 all the patients had been moved to Salisbury, so their information was out of date. What they ought to associate with Bethnal Green, he told his friends, was one of the oldest private charitable organizations in the country. In 1678, eight local property owners purchased land around the original estate, Bethnal House, and conveyed it to a trust. Under the terms of the trust, no one could build on the land, and the income from leasing it for grazing and gardening would benefit poor persons in the vicinity. "Poor's Land", it became, and for more than two hundred years, the trust had fended off others' attempts to purchase and build on the site. No doubt the founders of the charity were mainly concerned with preserving the view from their front windows, but nevertheless they had done something noble, and the charity survived. The land today, with only a few building additions (St. John's church and vicarage in the nineteenth century, the Museum Cinema and the Tube-station entrance in the twentieth), looked much as it might have in the seventeenth century, and the income still supplied the local poor with coal.

But if Laurie defended Bethnal Green and its high-minded history in one breath, he condemned it in the next. He thought the working classes an increasingly troubled lot. He sometimes harshly described the people who appeared in his court, but with an authority informed by experience. He saw them every day; he knew their local and domestic disputes, their confusions and misunderstandings, their habits and obsessions. What did his friends know, when they saw these people only on their occasional forays to the market in Covent Garden? And then did not even deign to make eye contact? As a metropolitan magistrate—part judge, part mediator, part counsellor—Laurie wanted to improve the lives of the poor.

Take, for example, a recent dispute before his court in Bow Street, in which a man stood accused of smashing lightbulbs and vandalizing the public surface shelters in his neighbourhood. Rather than punishing the man, Laurie asked why he was intent on this damage. Mr. Brimmer explained, rather eloquently, that he thought the government's standard of protection too low. He was forty-five years old, had fought in the first war, and followed the current one in the papers in great detail.

"Those shelters are safe from a five-hundred pound bomb only if it falls fifty feet away. What's the use of that?"

Laurie asked him if he could agree to put his argument in a letter to the home secretary, then redirect his energy to clearing bomb sites.

Mr. Brimmer eyed him, then agreed that he could. They shook hands, and Laurie enquired about his work. In good humour, Mr. Brimmer told him the family business was a bakery.

"Brimmer's Bread and Broken Bulkheads," Laurie said, knowing the alliteration would be joke enough. And indeed, Brimmer laughed.

Laurie looked across the fire at Armorel, wrapped snugly, stitching. Her skin was dry and red at this time of year, symptoms of a mild allergy to wool. "How's the landscape?" he asked.

Armorel and their daughter, Georgina, were members of a sewing circle preparing a section of a topographical quilt for the Royal Air Force. Folds and folds of material—shades of green and grey—covered the floors of their rooms, and Laurie found bits of thread on everything. The RAF insisted these "flexible landscapes", as they were known, were invaluable to pilots studying the terrain before bombing missions. Armorel's circle had been assigned the hills north of Hamburg, and sewing circles all over London had other portions of the map.

"How does a mother save her child in a crush like that? I don't understand the geometry of it."

"Armorel," he said.

"The sewing's fine. I've taken over Elizabeth Fulton's part."

"Why?"

"She's not on it anymore."

"I see. Had a falling out, did you?"

Armorel stopped sewing and looked at him. "Not at all. Toby's been killed."

"Oh, God."

He was their son's good friend. Andrew, also in the army, had known him since childhood. Laurie turned to the window and watched several crows balancing on the thin top branches of the plane trees in the park. Against the low sky, the birds seemed huge, ungainly. What was wrong with them? Did they grow larger in winter?

"Might that make her want to sew more?" he said. "For the war effort?"

Armorel wiped her eyes. "Not at the moment. That's just ridiculous."

"Where's Georgina?" He thought he knew but wanted the comfort of saying her name. For two months she'd been working for the Ministry of Information, living with several other girls near Bond Street, but she often came home for a night or two to sew and be under her mother's care. A series of respiratory illnesses had afflicted her since childhood. "I thought she was staying the night."

"She is. She's just gone down to the shops. They have oranges, apparently."

"Oranges," Laurie murmured.

Armorel smiled. "If it turns out to be true."

"I'm very sorry about Toby," Laurie said.

They looked at each other a moment, both thinking of Andrew.

"He's going to be fine," Laurie said. "I believe that."

"Please find out about the mothers," Armorel whispered. "And those babies."

Laurie turned back to his desk. He took out a sheet of writing paper and dashed off a note to the home secretary, agreeing to his request, but on slightly different terms.

Thirteen

Emma's funeral was at St. John's, and Rev. McNeely did the best he could. He hadn't known Emma well, and there was not much to say about the life of a four-year-old, he was discovering, that didn't fall into the category of innocence lost or adult regret. In his moth-bitten robe he spoke of her smile. He spoke of her devotion to Tilly. He spoke of her likeness to Ada. He did not mean to say how much her father, Robby, had wanted a boy when Emma was born, only how much he had loved his younger daughter, but this was his tenth funeral for a child under five, and, even with Psalm 23 read at each, he was having trouble keeping his mind clear. Anyway, the family was too far gone in grief to find fault with his words.

Ada and Robby stood in the front pew, Tilly between them. On 3 March, Robby had made it to the shelter. He'd been waiting for his family on the platform when the accident occurred. Ada had blamed him at first, said that if he'd come back for them instead of heading straight for the shelter from the Plots & Pints, everything might have been different. But Tilly had not agreed. Several times during the service, Ada reached for her shoulder. The girl didn't complain, but the stillness with which she greeted the pressure worried Ada.

They buried Emma in the churchyard of St. John's, a privilege granted by parish law to all families within the parish, regardless of religious affiliation. Three small graves, covered with fresh flowers, ended the row just behind Emma's. The flowers were the same—blue violets and white snowdrops, gathered from bomb sites—although the ceremonies had been quite different, two Jewish and one Catholic. When the service for Emma ended, when Rev. McNeely had said all the words the prayer book required, plus a few more of his own, and Tilly had tossed down the pouch of black draughts she wanted Emma to keep, the rain started. Everyone noted it, the way people always do when nature appears to take an interest in their lives.

At home Robby uncovered the sandwiches, and no one made jokes about that not being a man's work. The women took the cloths from him, put the kettle on, opened the back window, in spite of the rain, for air. No one had properly tended the flat since the accident. Ada, from a chair in the corner of the kitchen, asked her friends to sit and not worry. Ignoring her, they dampened cloths and went at the rooms with the energy of the lucky. "We'll put things right," they said.

In the small flat, Tilly didn't know where to go. The kitchen made her nervous. The lounge, where her father and his friends were drinking and growing loud, confused her.

"There are more refugees in the neighbourhood than ever before, aren't there?"

"Where was the bloody light?"

"You can bet they have a centre handrail at Kensington."

"They won't have a public inquiry because they know they'll be found out."

"When they say 'Jewish panic', do they mean they panicked or we did, about them?"

"I liked Mrs. W.," Tilly said abruptly. "She smelled of lavender."

Everyone stared. Then a neighbour, Mrs. Chase, knelt down. "That's nice."

Tilly looked at Mrs. Chase, unblinking. She had seen Mrs. Chase make faces many times behind Mrs. W.'s back.

"I didn't mind when she picked out her own vegetables," Tilly said. "It makes sense, doesn't it? If we were too busy to help her?"

Mrs. Chase turned to Robby. "Tilly has such beautiful skin," she said.

The men had brought pints from the local, and Robby's empty was being swapped for a fresh one. "Takes after her mother," he said.

Mrs. Chase saw no resemblance whatsoever but continued to smile agreeably. She turned back to Tilly and, suddenly inspired, attempted to match her demeanour. She dropped her smile.

"How brave you were, Tilly."

"We weren't brave. We—"

"Tilly," her mother interrupted from the kitchen. "Come here."

Mrs. Chase struggled to her feet while Tilly turned away.

"I heard Max Keeler was carried right along, his feet off the ground, his arms raised," one of the men said.

"Remind Keeler when he's out of hospital," said Robby. "Might inspire him to raise his wallet more often!" A burst of laughter filled the room.

In the kitchen, Ada pressed Tilly into a hug. Tilly tried to resist but couldn't. She sank to the floor with a sob, her head in her mother's lap. "I want Emma," she said.

Ada didn't speak but smoothed Tilly's hair with her palms.

Someone in the kitchen sloshed soapy water on the floor. Someone else threw a sponge at the back of a man who came in for more glasses. Tilly closed her eyes and pushed her forehead hard into her mother's leg, hard enough that Ada shifted. "Ouch. Tilly, stop now."

Tilly looked up.

Ada held her daughter's cheeks and wiped her tears with her thumbs. "What happened?" Tilly asked. Ada shook her head.

That afternoon Robby joined the mourners at St. John's. Many of his friends were there: Burnley, who'd lost both his children;

Hunt, who'd lost his wife, sister, and brother-in-law. Part of the group was talking about starting a petition for a public inquiry. Everyone was angry about the government's assumption that they'd accept a mass funeral. Thinking of that, Robby's knees nearly buckled. He swayed on the front steps, his cheeks streaked with tears the beer had released. The porch was fairly clean, given the constant gathering of people since 3 March. Someone had collected some fish-and-chip wrappers and stacked them in a corner beneath a stone. A dozen small bouquets lay soaked in the rain.

Some were saying that Max Keeler hadn't just raised his arms but had been passed over the heads of the crowd in the stairway so that he might help remove people from the bottom of the accident. His strength was legendary on the docks. Others said someone had climbed over the pile, but it wasn't Keeler; it was an off-duty police officer who'd done nothing to get the people out. The question rose again of a land mine, the sound that night, the missing bulb.

"Was it missing?"

"Yeah!"

"Burned out and never replaced!"

"What about a centre handrail? They've got them at Kensington."

"Bloody iron ones!"

Would a centre rail have helped? It didn't matter. It was compelling enough that the West End had them and the East End didn't.

"Where were the bloody wardens?"

"And the police? There was no constable at the entrance!"

Then someone mentioned the Gowers report, which had come hand in hand with the mass-funeral offer, and that was it. The crowd sparked. People jumped to their feet, swearing.

"They hushed up the inquiry!"

"The shelter's shit!"

"Why'd they tell us to bring the children home!"

"Emma!" Robby yelled. "Emma!"

His posture, slightly pitched forward, elbows out for balance, suggested determination to the largely inebriated gathering. The group rose behind him, mourners turned protesters turned organized crowd. All Robby had to do was raise his fist to elicit cheers of his name and Emma's. This was tantalizing, and he did it again and again. He led the crowd up Cambridge Heath, past the public baths and cinema, past the children's hospital, left on to Old Bethnal Green Road, to the police station. As they arrived in front of the dreary brick building, the sound of his dead daughter's name in the thick, damp air suddenly made him so angry, he kicked his foot through a car window. Then he fell backwards and knocked his head on the curb.

Fourteen

Just before dessert, the club's tent collapsed, the far end, away from Laurie and William. It happened slowly and softly, the two end poles falling away from the tables, so that the white tent settled over the luncheon like a blanket over a cradle. There were quite a few whoops and hollers. The men at the collapsed end scrambled quickly to escape; those at the other end stood and walked out relatively calmly. With the exception of Smith, who banged a knee against a chair while temporarily blinded under the tent, no one was hurt.

The members stood in groups about the lawn while the work of cleaning up began. Some had emerged with their drinks. New glasses appeared quickly for everyone else. Many told jokes about American manufacturing. Others discussed the relative merits of oak panelling versus white canvas as a form of shelter. One older member evaluated the experience against one of his in the RAF during the war; a younger member questioned what the debacle implied for the empire.

Without saying anything, the older members came to the same conclusion: the garden lunch had failed. Long live the grill room!

And the younger members decided they should give the tent another try but that in the long run the club would need an addition, a covered veranda of some sort. They proposed various fundraising ideas.

Laurie and William stood together in the sun, mostly silent.

The mishap had neither improved nor worsened Laurie's humour. He felt remote, numb. When he did speak to William, saying something about how small the space looked with the tent down, William was preoccupied with his shirt collar. It turned out a beetle was crawling there; he removed it and tossed it into the grass.

Once they were seated again inside, Laurie decided he would phone Paul Barber when he got home. He was staying at the B and B on the High Street, poor chap. He wouldn't find much to eat, Mrs. Loudon having become enamoured recently of the idea (and low cost) of the continental breakfast. But Laurie would cooperate with his film. That would feed the boy's enthusiasm, at any rate.

Had it really been thirty years? Laurie couldn't believe it. His fingers counted out the decades against his leg—'53, '63, '73. It was a habit, a dismal summary of the bulk of his life passing in a feathery movement of his fingers against his leg. He couldn't resist the chance to tell the story again, or at least play a role in what would inevitably be its new iteration. And that morning he'd done something new: he'd broken a rule of the Test and used more than one fly. His last cast before lunch, he'd tried Barber's clumsy lure and caught his biggest trout of the morning. His excited yelp had made Smith, that river muddier, lose his footing.

Inquiry

Fifteen

The tragedy does not remain the story. As with any other public property, it is transformed by use. What you want is a loved one, child, friend, to be found, safe, alive. That's not possible now. A few days earlier you might have accepted an apology from the government, or an explanation of what happened, or a promise that it would never happen again. But none of these things came about, and now you want someone humiliated, forced to resign. You want someone to admit responsibility, someone held accountable. Desperate for these things, grief hot in your blood, you stand on a cold curb in front of the town hall, chanting with the others who are there every day, "The light, the light," because to the crowd, the light is at the heart of the matter, the accident, the disaster, the catastrophe, whatever today's papers are calling it, the event that ended the lives they had and gave them new ones they never wanted and never will. All their misery, all their unmitigated despair at what their lives have become, reduced to two words.

As the inquiry began, winter rallied. Temperatures sank, and the radiators in the room were not up to the task. That first morning, a crowd gathered and watched Laurie arrive by cab, the way, he imagined, defeated villagers awaited their conquerors. They looked wary, but when Laurie stepped out and waved an arm in greeting, he needed the help of several constables to move through the sudden surge. They were not angry or violent, just insistent. Men called his name but were mute when he turned to listen. Women begged him not to forget the shelter orphans. They pulled back rough sleeves to show him their bruises, their children's bruises.

Laurie strove to be warm and cordial yet noncommittal.

The second-floor room he'd reserved for the inquiry was charmless, high ceilings and a wall of windows opposite the door its only attributes. Borough residents called it the marriage room because it was often used for civil ceremonies. Now, under a rolling blackboard, a pile of gas masks huddled like a small clan of burrowing animals. Stacked in a corner, several crates overflowed with donations for the shelter library, the pride of Bethnal Green. The room had burgundy carpeting and white walls splotched grey with damp. Cracks ran through the plaster ceiling, here and there a seam widening into a hole the way a stream feeds a lake. The place was freezing and dusty and in general smelled like a church.

"Quakers and conscientious objectors," explained Ian Ross, the Bethnal Green constable appointed Laurie's messenger for the duration of the inquiry. "They've held a few meetings here. With candles."

A small stage, just a foot and a half high, also carpeted in burgundy, anchored the far end of the room. Between Laurie and this stage stood a small sea of chairs. Most were wood, but a few upholstered ones, like royalty among the masses, had been dragged in as well. The uneven rows gave the room that first morning, Thursday, 11 March, the air of an amateur theatrical or a children's story hour rather than that of an official inquiry. The lights were dim, the curtains heavy, though someone had tied them back to let in what light there was from the street. The walls all around displayed hand-lettered signs about where families should go to collect the clothes and personal items of the victims.

"Where was Gowers' inquiry?" Laurie asked.

"Police station, sir."

Laurie walked to the windows and looked down. From here, the distance reduced the crowd, so animate and visceral when he'd arrived, to a nearly continuous layer of trembling black umbrella. Where there were gaps in the fabric, he saw a stoic, dripping face; pale, damp skin. He thought they had every right to be angrier than they seemed, and years later Laurie would say that the accident at Bethnal Green cried out for a more eloquent report than he thought he could write.

"These chairs," Laurie said, turning.

"A protest, sir," Ross said.

"Protest."

"It is the hope of the clerk who brought them in that the borough residents might storm the doors."

"And then be pleased to find a place to sit?" he said, smiling at Ross.

"Yes, sir. I believe there's one chair for every victim."

"What's his name?"

"Bertram Lodge."

"Ah." Laurie turned from the windows. "Well, they don't seem to mind standing out there." A few people had made signs.

"Also, sir, I'm to give you this." Ross held up a sealed envelope.

"Tell me."

"It's a letter from the Relatives' Committee. As you know, they're not being allowed to attend, so they wanted to submit to you a list of witnesses willing and able to testify on various points."

"Thoughtful."

Ross began stacking chairs. Laurie had written back to the home secretary, saying he wanted the authority to hold a public inquiry, and Morrison had responded favourably by morning post. By second post, however, after Laurie had already begun to make arrangements, Morrison insisted that the inquiry be private. The reason: secrets of home defence must not leak to the enemy. Laurie knew the real concern was morale. The War Office made nearly all decisions under its dull grey shadow. People like the anti-aircraft guns? Gives them a feeling of fighting back? Then it doesn't matter that the shrapnel kills more Londoners than German pilots. Morale was the altar on which reason was sacrificed every day. The assumption of victory was one of the government's cleverer tactics, most evident in the newspaper's daily reminders about the need to plan for peace. The officials would not accurately report the number of dead in the Bethnal Green accident, and they remained absolutely opposed to a public inquiry.

But Morrison wanted information. *How do the people behave? What is the nature of their trauma? Surely many will leave the area. Note the patterns of retreat and return.* Laurie had a letter in his briefcase outlining a dozen such queries. In their last conversation, Laurie had pointed out the irony of the shift. At first the accident hadn't happened; now they wanted to study it? Morrison made no comment.

"No," Laurie said, stopping Ross. "Leave the chairs. It will give the papers something to write about. They won't have much else."

Like a machine thrown into reverse, Ross immediately began unstacking the chairs, but something in his motion told Laurie he was pleased. Laurie needed an ally in the borough to call witnesses. Ross was tall and fit and looked well in his uniform; Laurie put a hand on his shoulder and assigned him the job. Then, clapping and rubbing his hands—partly for warmth, partly to test acoustics—Laurie walked to the front of the room.

He ordered a small table to be brought in. "Not a desk, not a dining table," he specified, and within the hour two constables found something appropriate in the mayor's office.

"Is the room adequate?" the mayor asked, trailing behind her confiscated table.

"Indeed," Laurie replied.

The mayor looked fondly at her side table. "I use it for tea," she offered, and then, as if this were perhaps too selfish for the times, added, "the clerks, too, borrow it now and then."

"Very good," Laurie said.

The mayor stood uncertainly. Morrison had not yet announced whether she would be permitted to attend the proceedings.

"Do you want to submit a written statement?" Laurie asked. He held up the envelope from the Relatives' Committee as precedent.

The mayor looked shocked. "Oh, no! No," she said, shaking her head. She would never be so much trouble. Then she appeared to reconsider. "Well, perhaps. Could I?"

"The sooner the better," Laurie said.

The mayor smiled but did not leave.

"Well," Laurie said, "if we need anything else, we'll know where to find you."

"Indeed," said the mayor. "With tea in my lap!" Then, fearing she'd been misunderstood, "Because of the table, of course."

"Of course," said Laurie.

After the mayor had gone, Ross discovered that the table had a wobble. "Perhaps the mayor has had tea in her lap on other occasions," he suggested.

"Our mission," Laurie said, "is to create an encouraging atmosphere. Everything different from what Gowers started. An inquiry at the police station. Imagine." He looked around the room. "A wobbly table shows we're making do, just as they are." He put a hand out and pressed the edge of the table. One of the legs clunked obligingly against the floor. "We want to be official in tone, helpful in mood. It's a powerful combination. We will sit here and here." Laurie pulled two wooden chairs forward and placed them on one side of the small table, angled as if for a fireside chat. "The witnesses will sit here." He pulled a soft armchair forward from the front row and set it facing the table, close enough that the witnesses could put their feet up if they wanted to.

"But I won't always sit across from them," Laurie said. "I'm going to move around a bit, and so are you." He pushed back some chairs in the front row of invisible demonstrators, gestured at the stage to indicate that it, too, was a seating option, and the arrangements were done. He wobbled the tea table again for good measure.

"No food," he said. "But let's have tea." Laurie turned to Ross. "Now?"

"No. This afternoon, when we start."

"Right."

Laurie stared at Ross and waited a moment. He gave the impression of choosing a course from several available options. He had, as always, only one in mind. "Let's go to the shelter," he said.

They left the town hall and walked down Cambridge Heath Road. A low fog skirted the trees and buildings and seemed to make the sounds of a still-stunned community ring louder. Laurie was surprised by the amount of anti-refugee graffiti he saw: various statements about the manners and vices of "four-by-twos". Crude opinions on "the Jewish problem". It made him quiet, but Ross talked all the way there.

"The shelter entrance is parallel to the line of the street, sir, but the stairs leading down lie at an angle."

Laurie would no doubt see that for himself. But the accident had occurred in a corner of Bethnal Green he didn't know well, and so he was willing to listen. His life tended north, along the eastern end of Old Ford Road and toward Approach Road, which led into Victoria Park. He and Armorel had been attending St. James's, off St. James Avenue, for years. Their butcher and greengrocer lay north. And when Laurie went for a walk, he was more likely to head into Victoria Park than south to Museum Gardens or the Bethnal Green Gardens, though he might have. They weren't far. He simply preferred the winding lanes and large lake of Victoria Park to the simple circle paths and paddling pools that filled the parks of Bethnal Green.

"Hard to imagine such a thing happening next to the church, sir," Ross was saying.

They arrived at the shelter, and Ross showed him the steps, pointed out how the first one, because of its relation to the pavement, was not of uniform width. "Could have been a contributing cause."

Laurie looked at Ross with an expression calculated to impress upon him the value of circumspection. Then he glanced quickly at the wooden gates, the corrugated iron roof, relieved to find no graffiti. Still, the flimsiness of the structure depressed him. There were more of the hand-lettered signs about collecting the victims' belongings, their black ink streaked with rain. In another hand, someone had written that tea and small sandwiches would be available.

Laurie and Ross descended to the landing at the turn in the steps to the booking hall. This was where the crush had occurred, and although the concrete had been scrubbed, there hung about the place a disturbing odour of urine mixed with damp and the smell of the garden above. Laurie quickly paced out the space and found it to be roughly fifteen feet by eleven. As he moved about, the gritty shuffle of his soles on the concrete bothered him. He found he could not escape an image of the fallen, interlocked bodies. He was a religious man and an orderly one, and he believed in the necessity of war, but death like this at home? He knelt by the steps and pulled out his measuring tape.

"Twelve inches deep, sir. Five and a half high."

Laurie swivelled and looked up at Ross.

"I took the liberty of measuring the stairs this morning, sir."

Laurie swivelled back. Plain concrete steps with a wooden edge, he noted. Fairly even, though the wood dipped slightly below the level of the concrete. Ross's numbers were exact.

"Well done," he said, standing, and Ross, embarrassed, shrugged.

Laurie pointed at the light socket above the steps.

"Empty," said Ross.

"Obviously," said Laurie.

"I mean, it's a bit of a controversy, sir. It was always dim. Some wanted it brighter, others wanted it dark until a more protected entrance could be built. I'm not sure, sir. I'd have to reserve judgement on that."

Laurie gave him a nod. "In general, a good idea."

In half an hour they made a cursory review of the rest of the shelter. Laurie was impressed by the library, built on cement slabs over the tracks. A small mullioned window gave it the appearance of an eighteenth-century shop, right there underground. Beyond it was a recreation hall, and at the other end of the platform, a nursery painted with bright murals. It was all quite extraordinary. He'd had no idea. Farther on, Ross showed him a canteen selling hot soup, cocoa, sandwiches, and cakes; two sick bays, one with a bathroom for delousing, the other with a rack of several dozen toothbrushes donated by the Junior Red Cross of America; and several nurses' stations. The whitewashed tunnels were fresh and surprisingly bright, triple-tiered bunks lining the walls on both sides as far as the eye could see. Well-posted signs gave polite directions and instructions to shelterers of all ages: *You are requested to be in your bunk by 11 p.m., as the floodgate closes at that time.* Laurie found himself nodding in approval. The underground life was better than he'd imagined, though when he looked at Ross, he saw him scowling.

"Very sad, sir," Ross said, "if you remember why most people come here. Many have lost a home, and a family member or two with it."

They walked back to the town hall in silence, Laurie watching the people on the streets, wondering which of them had been in the crowd that night. He thought of how afraid they must have been, their passage to the shelter mysteriously impeded. But with that fear, there must have been annoyance, mounting to anger, fuelled by exhaustion. He saw sleeplessness on every face.

Ross cleared his throat. "I wondered if I could be secretary to the inquiry, sir? Instead of messenger?"

Laurie pretended to consider a moment, then agreed.

Sixteen

Ada knew her grief was ugly, bloated. It bulged and spilled out of her. She could tell by the way visitors to the flat looked at her, looked and then looked away. All had been the future—tomorrow, after this raid, after the war. But now, sodden with sorrow, she was changing course. With every ounce of her body, she didn't want to take each day as it came, but she didn't seem to have any choice. All she wanted was a path back to the time when Tilly smiled and Emma napped on the pillow beneath the window.

She'd watched friends go through this, thought she had some idea, but she did not. It was painful to talk. The words, even when they sounded right, were slow in her head. She could never have imagined the agony of physical contact, the torture of a hug, except from Tilly, especially from Tilly. Now she knew the best thing to do for someone mourning, the only thing, was to bring food and leave.

At first she wanted to abandon Bethnal Green. Hadn't the government been trying to get them to the country from the beginning? Well, now she would go. She would banish herself. She could picture standing on the platform at Paddington, Tilly's hair neat and braided for the trip. She even got as far as pulling out the bag, but then she stalled. She started to cough and cry and ended up on her knees again, clutching Emma's pillow.

When she looked in the mirror, she saw that she was changing. She had a thin face now, eyes that didn't settle on anything for long. Days and events still ahead—peacetime, other mothers and daughters—would change her even more. She suspected she'd never get the feeling of 3 March out of her bones. It was like being in a fog and feeling every stinging raindrop. It was not a memory but a physical, altered state. One day the fog might clear, but she knew she'd been marked. She'd been seared. Perhaps one day she wouldn't even recognize herself.

The shelter orphans stayed at Bethnal Green Hospital for five days after the accident. All were healthy, if just a bit undernourished. "Who isn't?" Ada cried, shaking the newspaper. She clipped out all the stories she could find about the shelter orphans. The day the *Observer* announced that the babies were going to the orphanage in Shoreditch, Ada got out of bed, dressed, and filled her handbag. She was confused and disorganized with grief—everything took her a long time—but eventually she walked into the kitchen and found Tilly on her tiptoes, trying to tap down a box of salt from the top shelf with a butcher's knife. Ada surprised her, and the girl whipped around.

"You're up," Tilly said.

"You need a stool," said Ada.

"This works well, usually." Tilly put the knife back on the counter.

"What were you doing?"

"Checking the salt."

Ada walked to the shelf and pulled down the box. "It's about half-full."

"It's open, then. Dad said if it wasn't we should sell it."

"Why?"

"He's out in the shop, and he said it doesn't matter anymore what we eat."

"He's wrong about that."

"All right." Tilly didn't believe her, but she wanted to try.

"Do you want to come with me?" Ada asked. "I'm going to see the babies."

They waited for the city bus on the Roman Road, just east of St. John's. The entrance of the shelter, which a constable now guarded, had a new roof and reinforced doors. They didn't want to look there but couldn't help it. Several workers were installing an iron handrail down the centre of the stairway, and a group of people had gathered to watch.

The bus arrived. A few passengers got off, and when the crowd waiting at the stop tried to get on, Ada and Tilly fell back. There wasn't room for everyone. Suddenly furious with a woman who squeezed on ahead of them, Ada yelled something about four-by-twos. Frozen with fright, Tilly willed herself to forget the words almost the same moment she heard them. She couldn't move until Ada held her and said, "It's all right." But Ada, too, was shaking. Then the girl's face crumpled. She pushed her sob into her mother's side, and the bus pulled away.

"I'm sorry," Ada said.

"What does it mean?" If her mother said something, anything, else, Tilly would believe her.

"Nothing. We're going to walk."

"I like walking."

But Ada was not sure of the way. She had rarely been out of Bethnal Green. She knew from the papers that the Shoreditch orphanage was on the Bethnal Green Road, so if they stuck to it and kept west, she thought they'd be all right. She was glad the babies hadn't been taken to Kensington, as some had originally said. She never could have walked that far.

A layer of cloud still protected the city, but the noise of the street was too much for Ada, after her solitary days. She took Tilly's hand. A few streets later, she saw two magpies. "There you go," she said, giving Tilly a squeeze. "That's good luck, a pair of magpies." The birds were tussling over a shiny piece of tin in a garden.

"Do they have to be together?" Tilly asked.

Ada didn't answer.

"Is it still good luck if you see one and then a little while later you see another?"

"I think so."

"How long in between?"

"What?"

"Is it bad luck if you see just one?"

"I don't know, Tilly. Let's walk now."

"We are."

"Quietly, then. I need to think."

Twenty minutes later, mother and daughter stood before the orphanage. The proprietress—matron? Ada didn't know what to call her—welcomed them. Tilly only nodded in response to the woman's greeting. She wanted her mother to be able to think.

Seventeen

Paul arrived early wearing a jacket and dark tie, the most conservative he had. Dunne had been ambiguous on the phone about whether he intended to cooperate, but Paul thought he'd detected a developing curiosity and wanted to make a good impression. He could see Dunne through the front window, asleep in front of the television. He watched him for a time, surprised to feel sorry for the old magistrate. He looked vulnerable, head back, mouth open for air. When Dunne finally answered the door, sleepy but clearly pleased with the business of the day, Paul pretended he had not been waiting on the step for five minutes. He noted that, while he had made an effort to dress up for Dunne, Dunne seemed to have dressed down for him. He was wearing a cardigan and loose trousers over slippers. Once more, they proceeded slowly down the hall, Paul simultaneously loosening his tie and working hard to avoid stepping on Dunne's bare heels. When he slowed to the older man's pace, he noticed that the walls were lined with certificates and awards as well as a heavily textured green and grey quilt.

"Now," Dunne said when they were sitting down, "what will the point of this film be? What will you be trying to prove?"

Paul smiled. "Well, I've always been interested in—"

"Hosting a documentary."

"Not hosting it, sir. I probably won't appear at all, actually."

"Interviewing me, then."

"Someone else might film the interviews."

This news seemed to please Dunne.

"I'd write the script and direct the whole thing," Paul said defensively.

"Good for you."

"Yes, well, it would be, rather. I've wanted to make this film for a long time." Paul took a quiet breath. "Sir Laurence, my parents used to say you were the only one who understood the crowd wasn't guilty."

"Barber. It's a common name."

Paul thought Dunne meant uncommon for someone who looked like him. He was used to this. He had responses, jokes, a whole range of things he usually said. Now, though, he shrugged and tried to change the subject.

"As you know, the thirtieth anniversary is approaching, and many producers will find it a compelling time to look back."

"Thirty years."

"Hard to believe?"

"Why not the twenty-fifth or the fiftieth?"

Paul smiled again. "I see. Well, I suppose there is an arbitrary aspect, but if we wait until the fiftieth—" He stopped.

"Oh, I know I'm not going to live for ever. Of course, you always think death might make an exception for you, but so far I haven't seen any evidence."

Paul tried to start again. "The report, sir, came at such an interesting historical moment. I wonder if you could tell me—"

"When did you read it?"

"At university. I was twenty-two."

"So the subject is academic to you." Laurie frowned. "No, you said you grew up in Bethnal Green."

"That's right." Paul looked down, and when he looked up, his eyes were wide and innocent. "Sir Laurence, it's not academic for me."

"Oh?"

"My family was in the crush."

Dunne waited.

"I was adopted after the accident."

The magistrate didn't flinch. He merely blinked twice, then smoothed his legs with his palms from his hips to his knees. "That's very interesting," he said softly. "I thought the name was familiar. Did the family keep a greengrocer's?"

"Yes, for a time. My mum did after my dad left."

"Ada Barber."

"That's right. You remember her?"

"Where is she now?"

"She died a few years ago, I'm afraid."

"And Tilly?"

Paul was impressed. "She lives in Islington."

Dunne held his breath, then exhaled loudly. He stood up and switched off the television.

"Ada adopted one of the orphans," he said, facing away from Paul. "Why?" He turned around quickly. "Do you know?"

"I think our families were friends." Paul didn't understand the way Dunne was staring at him. His secret not having gone down the way he expected, he wasn't sure where they were now. "My understanding is that there was a terrible sense of communal guilt in the area after the accident."

"Do you know anything about your birth parents?"

"No. My mother said the orphanage kept very spotty records during the war. She had no love for the matron, apparently."

Dunne looked down. "Your parents said I knew the crowd wasn't guilty. Did Ada say that?"

"Yes."

"What's the opposite of guilty?" Dunne asked.

"Innocent?" Under Dunne's scrutiny, Paul couldn't suppress the question mark.

"Well, they weren't that, either."

Eighteen

Mrs. Barton-Malow, matron of the Shoreditch Orphanage for Babies and Children, was a heavy woman with a bounce in her step at odds with her large body. Ada didn't ask for a tour, but this was what Mrs. Barton-Malow assumed she wanted. And Ada, who wasn't sure what she wanted, found that following Mrs. Barton-Malow up and down the passages was easier than anything else. They looked into the girls' and boys' dayrooms, the cafeteria, the classrooms, everything broom clean but dull. Many women worked among the children at the orphanage, older women who seemed to touch the world more bluntly, the ends of their fingers round and soft from work. Their quiet, constant motion implied two things: everything needs care, and you don't have to be as gentle as you think. Just help. Change a pair of pants. Make a bed. Do what you can. At the end of the tour, Mrs. Barton-Malow showed them the small back garden, with its buried Anderson shelters, five of them in a row, so that the garden looked as though it had swallowed a serpent.

"We haven't had a casualty yet," Mrs. Barton-Malow said proudly. She turned to Tilly. "We're organized by age. You'd be in the one on the end there, I imagine. What are you? About ten?"

Ada waited for Tilly to correct her.

"Eight," Ada said, nudging Tilly.

The girl, unmoved, looked out at the shelter on the end.

"What about the babies?" Ada asked Mrs. Barton-Malow.

"Which ones, dear? We have lots."

Mrs. Barton-Malow began to walk back towards the girls' dayroom. Ada followed, and Tilly trailed behind her. When Mrs. Barton-Malow opened the door and ushered them in, Ada steered Tilly towards a group of girls playing a game of marbles, then joined Mrs. Barton-Malow back at the door. "It's the shelter orphans I'm curious about," she said.

"They're in the nursery now, with all the other babies."

"Have any been adopted?"

"Not yet, despite all promises to the contrary." Mrs. Barton-Malow sighed. "We agreed to take them—we were already at capacity, mind you—only because we were promised they'd be adopted in a hurry. Public sympathy running high, they said. Well, not high enough."

Sudden, wild laughter caught her attention, and Mrs. Barton-Malow turned sharply towards the room. She rapped her knuckles on the door frame, and the children were quiet. Then she took Ada's arm and moved her a step farther into the passage.

"Anyway, 'Give it time,' they said." Mrs. Barton-Malow scrunched up her nose to show what she thought of that idea. "In my experience, that's not how time and sympathy work."

Ada shook her head. She'd never thought to have an opinion on the pair.

"I'll tell you what time does do," Mrs. Barton-Malow continued, leaning down to press a piece of broken tile into the floor. "It makes things harder to fix."

When Mrs. Barton-Malow stood up, her cheeks were flushed. "Might have all passed over if they'd kept it out of the papers, but now we have a real mess. I guess that's what you get when you offer sweets to children."

"Money," Ada said.

"What?"

"I thought it was money they offered." She looked for Tilly, still playing marbles. "That's what I heard, anyway."

"The point is, time weakens people. Their sympathy, courage, what have you."

"What I came about," Ada said, making an effort to sound friendly, "is the shelter orphans. I'd like to see them, if I could."

"I don't know how you expect me to know those babies from all the others, but if you'd like, I'll take you to the nursery."

"Yes. Thank you." Ada turned to get Tilly, but Mrs. Barton-Malow stopped her.

"Older children are not allowed," she said. "The possibility of contagion is too great."

Ada's eyes filled suddenly. "Can't you make an exception?"

Mrs. Barton-Malow raised her eyebrows.

"We were in the crush!" Ada said. "I had another daughter, who died."

Mrs. Barton-Malow patted Ada's hand. "And her sister is taking it very hard and wants to see the babies?"

Ada nodded and, turning, was startled to see that Tilly was standing right behind her.

"Shall we?" said Mrs. Barton-Malow.

It seemed Mrs. Barton-Malow had been disingenuous. In the nursery, a row of seven cribs stood apart from all the others. In fact, they were nearly partitioned off by a wall of boxes overflowing with stuffed animals, clothes, toys, bottles, and tins of milk and food. On every box someone had scrawled *3/3 Orphans*. It was the neatest room they'd seen so far and, though dimly lit, smelled of soap and warmth. Several babies were gently snoring.

"Are any of them Jewish?" Ada asked quietly.

Mrs. Barton-Malow raised an eyebrow. "One of the boys is circumcised, if that's what you mean."

Ada passed by each crib. She would have known anyway—there was a strong resemblance to his mother in his lips—but she glanced over at Mrs. Barton-Malow to confirm. Yes, Mrs. Barton-Malow nodded. That was the circumcised boy.

When Ada picked him up, she remembered Emma: a heartbeat, the smell of milk, a hand tucked into hers whenever she permitted it.

Standing next to her mother, her cheek on the baby's blanket, Tilly remembered Emma's smile, her blue coat in the snow.

Mrs. Barton-Malow stood by the window. Her only child, a boy, had died in the fire raid the first year. She looked out of the window—double glazed in here to make the room warmer for the babies, her own design—and saw a pair of dead bumblebees between the panes. They were furry and ancient, bleached white by the sun. Mrs. Barton-Malow opened the inside window, had to shove hard to unstick it, and angrily swept them up in her hand. She was sorry for herself, for Ada, for all the mothers the war had damaged. When she turned back to Ada, she said, "Why are you here?"

Ada's eyes were full of tears. "I thought it would help."

"Ah, well. It does help some. Depends what kind of person you are."

Nineteen

Laurie opened the inquiry the afternoon of Thursday, 11 March 1943.

"There is something I think it is probably my duty to mention," he began. In the room with him were Ross, secretary to the inquiry, and a stenographer, Mrs. King, from the local school. "There will be matter given in evidence that is strictly confidential, and of course any improper use of that material would constitute an offence under the Defence of the Realm regulations." Ross and Mrs. King nodded.

"Now let's call and examine the first witness."

As it was not a court, Laurie found it desirable to vary some of the usual procedures. There was no procession. The witnesses were kept across the hall in the small office of Mrs. Mallory, who typed requests for building repairs in the borough. In the days that followed, Mrs. Mallory fell into the habit of engaging all the witnesses in conversation. Ross often had to wait a few minutes while she jotted down a name or finished giving a piece of advice. A number of times he had to insist that Mrs. Mallory release a witness from a hug.

"Lord knows they need this more than anything else," she said.

"You are feeling below the mark?" Laurie asked. He wanted to be kind at the beginning.

"I am very much below the mark, sir."

"Is this owing to the shock of what happened?"

"Yes, sir. I worked up to the last before I went down to the first aid, and this is how it has left me." The man was pale and shaking. "The doctor has ordered me to go to a place where it is very quiet."

"Very wise. Let me just turn up your statement, and we will try to be brief. Now, your name is Henderson?"

"That is right."

"And you are a constable at the Bethnal Green Police Station, H Division?"

"That is right."

"What is your full name?"

"Martin, sir. Henderson."

"Where were you when the alert sounded?"

"We were in a desperate position, sir. We thought we could not do anything outside until the pressure was removed inside, you see."

"Now you're getting ahead of me. Let us just take it by stages. Where were you when the alert sounded?"

"On patrol, sir."

"What are your instructions in an alert?"

"To get to the shelter entrance."

"Were you able to do that?"

"Yes, sir."

"This particular night, the third of March?"

"Yes."

"When you got to the entrance, what was happening?"

"I saw men working there as I have never seen men work before. They were crying because they were so desperate. We could not extricate the people."

"So when you arrived, something had already gone wrong?"

"Yes, sir."

"What did you do?"

"I was directed by my superior officer to get over the crowd and work from the bottom. We thought it would be simpler from the bottom."

"You got over the people on the stairs, did you? How?"

"I swung from a girder. I accidentally kicked one or two people, but it couldn't be helped. From the top it looked as if it would be much simpler to get at them from the bottom, but when you got to the bottom, it looked simpler from the top. It was actually much worse from the bottom."

"They were filling the landing, I imagine?"

"No one was on the landing."

"But they must have been pressed against that far wall?"

"No, sir. It was very dark, of course, but I can tell you no one was on the landing. That's where I and several other people stood to try to get them out."

"Have you ever known any trouble of this sort before at the shelter?"

"No, sir."

"No panic or disorder at the entrance?"

"None whatsoever, sir."

"You are the superintendent of H Division?"

"Yes."

"And that includes the whole area affected by this tragedy?"

"Yes, sir."

"What is the area roughly served by the shelter—could you tell me that?"

"Mainly this end of Bethnal Green. I think most of the shelterers live in Bethnal Green."

"What would it involve, the longest walk for a resident to get to the shelter in the area served? A quarter of a mile, half a mile, that sort of thing?"

"Ten minutes at the outside."

"Ten minutes would cover it?"

"Assuming a person could walk half a mile in ten minutes."

"You have been in charge of this division since before the war. Has there been any similar incident in the division?"

"No, sir."

"Generally the population behaved well during the Blitz?"

"Extremely well."

"And since?"

"Yes, very well."

"There was a good deal of expectation, I suppose, that there would be a retaliation that night."

"Yes, quite a deal."

"Do you think the people were jumpy?"

"I would not say jumpy. They were expectant. We all were."

"You had difficulty in getting the pile sorted, in getting the people away from the entrance?"

"It was nearly impossible to sort out which person was free to be removed. I am at a loss to account for it. I did not think it was possible for people to get so mixed up that it would be impossible to lift them off one by one."

The work suited Laurie's manner and physique. He had a penchant for seeming to understand even when he didn't—this reassured his witnesses—and he was good at asking a lot of questions until he did. He held his hands in front of him, often touching his fingertips together in the shape of a vaulted ceiling. If he was at a loss for words, he sometimes rubbed his neck as if he had a sore muscle. The four prominent lines running parallel across his forehead tended to knit themselves in consternation during the hardest interviews but always unravelled for a joke. From his clothes and background, he knew they expected academic pretension, and he hoped they were surprised when they got conversational warmth. He wanted them to know that he, like they, had not left the city at the start of the war. This was certainly a mark in his favour.

———

"When you arrived, were other officers and wardens already working there?"

"Two constables, I believe. I didn't see any wardens."

"That was at your end?"

"That was at my end."

"That was the lower end, inside the shelter?"

"Yes."

"You came by way of the emergency exit?"

"That is correct."

"And you saw no wardens in tin hats?"

"No, sir. It was very dark, though."

"And when you got to the bottom of the stairs, was there difficulty removing the people?"

"There was terrible difficulty in extricating the bodies."

"Why was that? Why couldn't you just take them away one by one?"

"It is rather difficult to explain. The only way I can describe it . . ." The witness stopped a minute. "If we imagine my fingers as being about two hundred and fifty people, they were just like this." He clasped his hands, fingers tightly interlaced, then twisted and turned his wrists until it looked like he might be hurting himself.

"I see. They were all wedged up like that, were they?"

"It was impossible, sir."

"And the pile shifted forward from the bottom step, on to the landing, I imagine?"

"No, sir. No one was on the landing."

"You are an officer at Bethnal Green Station?"

"That's right."

"Had you or any of the other officers ever anticipated anything like this happening?"

"No, sir. We've had a little trouble, ordinary trouble, but nothing like this."

"What is the sort of trouble you have had?"

"It is a very mixed crowd, sir, all nationalities here, so just the ordinary sorts of clashes. There are the blacks, the Yiddish people, Maltese, Chinese, every kind down there, and when you get a crowd of that description, you are bound to have a little disorder."

"I see. Have you found much difference in the behaviour of the different races?"

"Not particularly."

"One is as easy to control as any other?"

"Most of the time, sir."

"And yet a mixed crowd like that has clashes."

"In my experience, sir."

Laurie remained poised but friendly, engaging but not eager. He was taller than many of the East Enders, but because he was thin, they could tell themselves he lacked strength. This was far from true, but unimportant. During breaks, he walked the streets and studied the poor condition of the dwellings. He'd already taken note of the worn and mended clothing, the blue and grey best clothes the Bethnal Greeners wore to come before the inquiry. He didn't expect to be invited in, and he wasn't, but he knew that many families with several generations lived in no more than two or three rooms, sometimes with boarders. To Laurie, this proof of their already cramped lives made the crush even crueller.

"In your opinion, did the different races or nationalities or creeds or denominations we have here play any role in it?"

"No, sir."

"No difference in behaviour, then, that you've noticed?"

"Well, I do know that it is necessary for the Jew to wail. I didn't know that before."

"I see. How long have you lived in Bethnal Green?"

"My whole life, sir.

Twenty

"Could you tell me more about the room?" Paul asked. The windows were open on to the garden. They'd been talking for an hour, and Paul had been invited to stay for lunch. He hoped they might eat outside.

"Many attributed your success with the East Enders to the casual atmosphere you created."

Dunne smiled.

"The table, for instance. A small one, arranged as if at a club."

"I liked that table. So did the mayor, as I recall."

Paul studied his notes. It was their second day of interviews, and he couldn't tell if Dunne was being serious or not. Since Dunne had learned he was one of the orphans, their conversations had eased but not deepened. The old magistrate seemed amused by his questions, as if reminded of an old joke or a favourite childhood friend, and Paul felt a bit lost. He tried another direction.

"Let me ask you about the opening of the report. Stylistically, it was an unusual choice, and yet it gave the report a wide popular appeal."

"When it was published."

"Yes. Was that your hope, that it would have popular appeal? Were you trying to set a precedent for future government reports?"

Dunne tilted his head in thought. "Good questions. Let's eat first, and I'll try to think of answers."

Paul followed him to the kitchen. A loaf of bread was set out, still in its plastic sleeve, next to plates, napkins, wineglasses—all mismatched from several ornate sets. Slices of cheddar and roast beef were displayed unceremoniously in their wrappers.

"A luncheon buffet," Dunne said, gesturing to a chair. "I thought we'd fend for ourselves. What would you like to drink?"

There was no room on the small table for Paul's notebook, so he slid it under his chair, surprised to find the floor sticky. Dunne poured two generous glasses of wine and offered him the bread.

"Help yourself."

He brought over mayonnaise and mustard, an avocado, and a bag of carrots. Paul smiled and assembled his lunch a step behind Dunne in order to understand the rules. When Dunne used his fingers to peel off a piece of roast beef, so did Paul. When Dunne used the same knife for the mayonnaise and the mustard, so did Paul. He would have liked a slice of avocado, but Dunne's peeling of it made such a mash, Paul declined. Dunne had nearly finished his glass of wine before the sandwiches were complete.

"Bon appétit," Dunne said, lifting his sandwich with one hand, pouring more wine with the other.

Paul took a bite, chewed, and swallowed. Never had he felt less hungry.

"Are you married?" Dunne asked.

Paul shook his head.

Dunne regarded him with affection. "Don't wait too long. Oh, well, do whatever you want. I can see you're trying to make something of yourself. Good for you. Now's the time."

Paul looked down at the mess of his sandwich. He wasn't sure what Dunne was talking about, but he hoped to find a way back to the report. "It's been almost thirty years since the accident," he tried.

"You keep reminding me."

Paul wiped his mouth. "You faced an impossible task—

to make sense of a pointless tragedy—and within three weeks you interviewed eighty witnesses and wrote a full report yourself. That would be inconceivable today. Today it would take two weeks merely to decide on the members of the investigating commission." He stopped, but Dunne's pleased expression encouraged him. "Then there's the writing itself. It's artful and compassionate—the opening, especially, of course. The story I want to tell is how and why you told the story of the tragedy the way you did."

"Death demands ceremony. An inquiry is just a kind of ceremony."

Paul shook his head. "The inquiry, yes. Call it ceremony. But not your report. It was something else."

"I wanted it to be. I did have this idea that the people should read it, needed to read it." He took a small foil-wrapped cake out of the refrigerator.

"And with the almost novelistic opening you gave them, they did." Paul reached for his tape recorder, thought it might be all right now, but Laurie shook his head.

"Another angle that interests me," Paul continued, setting the tape recorder back down, "is that the first woman to fall was never identified."

"Angle," Laurie said, and Paul could tell he'd used the wrong word.

"Perspective. Maybe I just mean detail. It was widely known at the time that a woman was the first to fall. But she was never identified, right?"

Laurie was silent.

"Is there something we don't know?"

Dunne fussed with the foil around the cake a moment, then gave up. "Yes."

Paul stopped chewing.

Dunne picked up a knife and began sawing into the cake

through the foil. "I've always thought of reports as the gospels of our time. The way they authorize a particular version of events."

"That would make you the messenger," Paul said.

"Oh, I didn't mind that," Dunne said. He served Paul a pile of cake crumbs. "The first woman to fall was a refugee."

Twenty-one

"What is the shelter's rate of intake, normally? How long does it take to get, say, six thousand people down?"

"I should think fifteen to twenty minutes. Three to three-and-a-half minutes a thousand. That is what I would estimate."

"That is something over two per second passing a given point on the escalator?"

"Yes."

"That is a good many, is it not?"

"They go through very quickly. The speed is quite good."

"I see. Is it your opinion that nationalities, races, creeds, denominations, played any part in this at all?"

"Not in this, no."

"Have you ever noticed, as a matter of interest, any difference in behaviour between the different nationalities or races we have here?"

"I cannot say that I have. Of course, we have here at Bethnal Green a lot of the fellow we call the Cockney, the real good old Cockney, and I think that is why we have little panic here. But even the Jew, contrary to what we believed, stood up to it pretty well. They surprised me and everybody else who knows this part of London."

"You were in the crowd outside the shelter the night of the third of March?"

"Yes."

"What did you see when you arrived?"

"It was very dark. The crowd was moving along all right down the stairs, and suddenly the people in the front seemed to stop, and I felt an awful pressure from the back."

"You couldn't go forward and you couldn't go back?"

"That's right."

"And you didn't know why you couldn't go forward. Did anybody seem to know?"

"No."

"Could you see down the staircase at all?"

"Not really."

"Did any of the people seem to be seeing down the staircase?"

"No."

"What were the people doing?"

"How do you mean?"

"What were they doing, how were they behaving?"

"We were waiting. Some people were worried. We thought the bombs had started."

"Why?"

"People yelled they'd started dropping them."

"Who yelled that?"

"I don't know."

"How long do you think you were there?"

"I should think ten minutes."

"But everybody is all right?"

"The baby came through. I lost my two oldest."

"Where was your husband?"

"I was talking to him and trying to pull him out, right at the bottom of the stairs."

"He was at the bottom?"

"Yes, right at the bottom. All he was saying was, 'Get Ivy out!'— she's our baby—and luckily someone did pull her out for me."

"But your husband, unfortunately—"

"No, he is in hospital."

"Oh, that's good. What is the matter?"

"He says he cannot feel his legs."

"I expect the doctors will patch him up all right."

"Of course, I lost my mother and two sisters."

"I am interested in the first woman who is supposed to have fallen. You say you saw her?"

"Yes, sir."

"Did you know her?"

"No."

"Do you know what happened to her?"

"No, sir."

"Did you see her afterwards? Did she make it out of the heap?"

"I don't know, sir."

"You live at Seventy-one Royston Street, Bethnal Green?"

"Yes."

"Where were you when the alert sounded?"

"Indoors with my three little ones."

"At home?"

"Yes."

"What did you do?"

"I gathered up what I could and ran with the children to the shelter."

"You ran, did you?"

"Yes."

"How old are the children?"

"One is three and a half, the next one is six, and the other one is eleven."

"Let me ask you right away, because the notes I have are not always accurate about this: the children are all right, are they?"

———

Laurie ate a cold Woolton pie that night with Armorel. He told her some of the stories he'd heard. "The victims looked alive until a warden touched them. Then they disintegrated."

Armorel shook her head.

"The result, they say, of a new bomb that takes the breath out of people. Some took the bodies of their children home with them, convinced that the government, for unspecified reasons, wouldn't allow them a proper burial."

"Oh, Laurie."

He told her that many of the witnesses mentioned a sound, something they heard that night that was different. They described it variously as a screaming blast, a crack, a rocket. What was clear in all cases was that it had made no sense to them. The East Enders knew the nightmare of aerial bombardment: the sirens, the drone of aircraft, the rumble of guns. They had nicknames for the searchlights and the barrage balloons, the pilots and the bombs. They claimed to be able to gauge by sound alone the location of a bomb, exploded or unexploded, incendiary, oil, or high explosive.

"Do you believe them?" Armorel asked.

"About this, I do."

"Then I do, too. That night they must have heard something."

"But when, exactly? That will be important. Anyway, I have a good lad helping. Ian Ross, a local constable. Quite capable, I think."

Armorel put down her fork. "Isn't it remarkable?" she said.

"What?"

"There is always such a supply of capable young men around you, and yet the city complains of a shortage."

"If you're worried about Andrew, remember you're also proud. He's going to be fine."

Armorel shook her head again and picked up her spoon. "This is just soup with a crust. Do you think Lord Woolton eats it?"

Laurie smiled. Like most of their friends, they'd dismissed their servants for war work and now managed on their own. Woolton pie was supposed to count towards making your main dish a potato dish three times a week, according to the Ministry of Food's Potato Plan. "I read the other day that crockery breakage is down ninety per cent," he offered.

"Yes, and indigestion is up a hundred," replied Armorel.

Laurie took another bite of the tasteless soup. "The mayor's an odd woman," he went on, "but I don't think she'll be any trouble."

"Did you choose this Ross, or was he assigned to you?" Armorel asked.

"I chose him. He seems intelligent."

"Should we have him to dinner?"

"I don't think that will be necessary."

"I mean, would you like to have him to dinner?"

Laurie shook his head, his thoughts returning to the day's testimony: "A few witnesses insisted on telling me the story of how they escaped being in the wrong place at the wrong time. Infuriating. Don't they know a near miss is always safe enough?"

Twenty-two

After the orphanage, mother and daughter suffered a reversal. Tilly lay in bed now, while Ada moved about the flat. Tilly could hear her mother's knees and ankles popping as she cleaned at night, her dull humming as she started taking care of the kitchen again and preparing the window boxes for vegetables. Her father was busy in the greengrocer's, his work ethic as improved by the fall, her mother said, as his comprehension was diminished. Now and then, Ada came to the bed and pulled Tilly close. She touched her cheek to the top of her head, so that Tilly felt like a baby bird tucked under a wing—that press of comfort, wordless. When it worked, Tilly fell asleep. When it didn't, Tilly held her breath so as not to have her mother's scent in her nose.

Rev. McNeely visited. At first Tilly thought it was a condolence call, but as she listened to their conversation from the bedroom, she realized her mother had asked him to come.

"I think I could endure anything," she said. "I'm not even scared. If I died I would miss Tilly, but I feel as though I have a child on each side of an abyss now and death would be just crossing over to spend time with the one I haven't seen in a while."

When Tilly pulled herself up on the pillow, she could see Rev. McNeely's face through the doorway, beyond her mother's shoulder. She startled him, and he spilled some tea on his hand. Her mother said, "Quick, pinch your earlobe."

He stared at Ada, his burned fingers pressed into the opposite palm.

"It takes the heat and your ear doesn't feel it."

He did as he was told. After a moment he said, "About your question." He spoke softly, but Tilly could make out most of what he said. "According to parish law, anyone residing within the parish is entitled to the sacrament of baptism, regardless of race. Marriage and burial, too."

"That's good," her mother said. "And godparents?"

"Of course. If they agree."

"Would you?"

There was another silence.

"Do you mean as a matter of principle, or are you—"

"I don't know who else to ask."

Now Tilly knew why her mother had set the table with their best cloth. She offered more tea, but McNeely declined.

"I see. Well, yes, it is an interesting question, isn't it?"

Ada waited.

"If you needed me," McNeely said, "of course. But perhaps you'll think of someone else."

"I don't think so."

"It must be very hard, Mrs. Barber."

"I got Tilly out."

McNeely nodded vigorously. "Of course. And with time . . ."

Her mother shook her head and closed her eyes. After a minute she continued as before. "Time has nothing to do here. Two is what I'm used to."

Rev. McNeely took a last sip of tea. He had to go. He had another funeral at the church.

At the door her mother thanked him for coming.

"I hope I've been of service, if perhaps not a comfort."

"Yes, thank you."

McNeely stopped in the doorway. He was only a bit taller than her mother, but it seemed to Tilly he looked down on her from a great height with kindness. "Ada," he said, "you can always come to see me privately if there's something more to discuss."

Tilly was as surprised as he to see her mother begin to shake.

Twenty-three

"Before you headed to the shelter, Mr. Steadman, was there anything you had to finish up in the Bricklayers' Arms?"

"I was drinking a pint, sir."

"And you dealt with that, I trust?"

"I drank my pint right up."

"Good man."

Bill Steadman, a fifty-year-old pensioner wearing a police-issue vest, explained that he'd been concerned about a heavy flow of people that night and was serving as a volunteer.

"I often did so, sir. My heart, it dislikes the damp. Warden Low was always kind enough to let me stay in the booking hall, so I tried to be of some use."

"And were you wearing this at the time?" Laurie indicated the vest.

"No, sir. I got this after the accident. I've become more official at the shelter since the night in question."

"I see. Well, you're fortunate it's just your heart dislikes the damp. My whole body is rather indisposed to it," said Laurie. He expected a chuckle.

"Do you often go to the public shelters?" Steadman asked.

Steady man, Laurie thought. Earns his name. "Perhaps not," Laurie said. He resisted the urge to sit straighter, remained deliberately at ease. "So, what did you see from this less inclement vantage point?"

Steadman hesitated.

"After the rain, the night was clear," Laurie said, prompting him. "There are rumours of a reprisal; the alert sounds; people begin to go in."

"There were a lot of children, sir," Steadman said.

"Yes."

"And we'd heard there'd be less time if they used some of the new bombs."

"The crowd was coming down perfectly normally. When did you know there was trouble?"

"The people stopped, sir. Suddenly there was no one at the escalator."

"Then what?"

"There was a scream."

"Where from?"

"From the crowd."

"Where was the crowd?"

"On the nineteen stairs."

"Anybody on the landing?"

"No one was on the landing."

Laurie shook his head. How could no one have been on the landing? What were they pressed against, if not the far wall?

"A woman fell, sir. That's what started it."

"I've read that. What happened to her?"

"I don't know, sir. I've tried everybody down the Tube to find out who she was."

"Women must have stumbled on the stairs frequently," Laurie suggested.

"Yes, but the crowd was moving along all right until then."

Laurie waited.

"She just fell. That's all. I couldn't say how, exactly, but that was the beginning of it."

"Why didn't she get up?"

"She couldn't. She was carrying a large bundle. I really couldn't say how she fell, but there were so many people coming, they tripped right on top of her, one after another. I helped some of them, but . . ."

"Did you succeed?" asked Laurie.

"It happened so fast. People fell everywhere, and we couldn't get anyone loose." His eyes went shiny. He pushed hard at his cheek with the fingertips of one hand, then repeated the gesture on the other side. Tears trailed down. "I've never seen anything like it. There was one man who turned around. I wasn't sure if he'd changed his mind or—no, I think he saw what had happened and wanted to hold back the crowd. He held up his arms, but he was pushed backwards and down, too."

"Was this before or after the blast many heard?"

"I didn't hear anything, sir."

"But you were in the stairway."

"Yes."

"And you didn't hear an unusually loud sound or blast that night?"

"No, sir."

"Did you see any of these babies? The shelter orphans we've heard so much about?"

"Yes," Steadman said. "I received most of them!" He covered his face with his hands.

"What do you mean?"

"I reached for them. They were just there; I don't know how. The people were packed in so tight, arms and legs all tangled up. It was the strangest thing, but some of those babies were passed forwards, and I reached for them. God knows how. I put my head under someone to get a baby in very dark clothes. Who the baby belonged to, I don't know. Possibly it went with that first woman who fell."

"She was carrying a baby?" Laurie looked at Ross.

"I couldn't be sure, sir. As I said, I didn't see how she fell, exactly."

"Right. Well, what did you do with them?"

"The babies? I laid them down by the escalators."

"How many were there?"

"More than a dozen."

"Not seven?"

"By the next morning the families had claimed some of them."

"And the others?"

"I imagine those are the orphans."

Laurie, Steadman, and Ross were silent. Then Laurie said, "Good man. It can fairly be said you did succeed."

"Oh, no," Steadman protested, his eyes filling again. "It was the mothers' doing. I just reached for them."

"You are James Low?"

"Yes."

"You are chief shelter warden of the Tube-station shelter in this borough?"

"I was. Sir, may I speak first?"

Looking at his hands, he told them that on the night of 3 March, he'd replaced the twenty-five-watt bulb above the stairs with one of a significantly higher wattage—an improvement he'd thought necessary, given certain structural problems with the shelter's entrance and the wet, slippery steps. What had happened, he believed, was that a couple of the first shelterers, approaching the entrance after the blackout, noticed the brighter light and smashed it on their way down. They would have done this out of worry that some light would reach the pavement outside during the blackout.

When Laurie didn't respond, Low said, "I'm sorry. I should've known they'd do it. I know how they think. We'd always hoped for a better entrance so that we could allow more light on the stairs."

The room smelled of tea and damp. A light rain fell outside on the street. Laurie wasn't sure what to do with Low's recitation of guilt. Certainly the man before him seemed broken. His eyes looked hot, which belied his outward calm. He might be sick, Laurie thought, or sedated.

"When I saw the shelter this morning," Laurie said, "the socket was empty."

Low nodded.

"Some seem to believe there was no light at all, and I did notice there was no broken glass."

"The clean-up was organized very quickly," Low said. "The Regional Commissioners had sweepers in before dawn." He did not sound defensive, only matter-of-fact.

Laurie looked at Ross, who stood and poured Low a cup of tea. Then, instead of returning to his chair, he perched himself on the edge of the stage.

"Regardless," Laurie said, "I'm not sure of this light's overall significance."

Low looked stunned. "Our regular habit at the shelter, sir, is to use a twenty-five-watt bulb. I'm afraid sixty-five watts would have struck many as too bright."

"Lightbulbs in doorways are always being smashed. It's practically war work for men of a certain mind-set."

Laurie asked about shelter size, regulations, staffing, maintenance.

"Who was on duty on the third?"

"Myself; the deputy warden, Hastings; and four part-time wardens, Edwards, Bryant, Clarke, and Bagshaw."

"What were their posts?"

"Clarke and Bryant were at the top of the escalator."

"Your post, naturally, is in the office?"

"Yes."

"Where was your deputy, Hastings?"

"He was in the office with me."

"Bagshaw?"

"Bagshaw was at the bottom of the steps in the booking hall."

"There is a man called Steadman who apparently is not a warden but was helping?"

"He's a volunteer. He has been very useful."

"And he stands in the booking hall?"

"Yes, at the bottom of the stairs with Bagshaw."

"And who was at the top of the stairs?"

"Edwards."

"You are satisfied with your wardens? You are satisfied they were at their posts?"

"Yes. They're good men. They know their jobs and work hard."

Laurie moved on to possible contributory causes.

"What about Constable Henderson, the police officer who should have been at the entrance?"

"A good man, tired of his job," Low said.

"What about this idea that it was a Jewish panic?"

"Absolutely not. Not too many Jews were in the habit of using this shelter."

"Why is that?"

Low looked embarrassed. "We had a bit of trouble in the beginning."

"Trouble?"

"Just the ordinary sort. Bullying, you know. But it had got much better. When the bunks came in and the walls were painted, it got easier. We haven't had a problem in some time."

"What accounts for this rumour, then?"

"My opinion? The large amounts of money found in a few of the handbags. That got into the papers, and people made their own assumptions."

Laurie nodded. In one case £750 was found. That bag belonged to a shopkeeper taking the day's takings straight to the shelter.

"Was there worry in the borough about future air raids?"

"Yes, but with light on the stairs, we would have been fine."

"Any gates closed or locked?"

"Not at the entrance."

"Are there orders issued or instructions about people being allowed to bring in large bundles?"

"No, we have never prevented them from bringing bedding. Some of them do bring enormous bundles with them. Generally speaking, we avoid that as much as possible by allowing people to leave their bedding. People who use the shelter regularly can leave their bedding there, provided they keep it in a clean condition."

"And the number of babies passed out? The seven so-called shelter orphans?"

"What?" Low shook his head in disbelief. "I haven't heard about that."

"Have you read the papers?"

"No, sir." Low looked out of the window, his eyes beginning to fill. "My wife says she smiles more than all the children she sees. She says that proves, if nothing else does, that something is wrong with the world."

Laurie nodded. "I'm much obliged to you, Mr. Low. Thank you for your help. If we need anything else, you'll come back and talk to us again?"

"I certainly would."

After Low withdrew, Ross told Laurie how respected Low and his wife were. "He tried to give the air-raid protection schemes a good name back when they were still a joke. He tries to be, you know, not too officious. Rather than constantly supervising, he establishes responsibilities and assumes his staff will follow through. That's easy to regret after a tragedy, but it's not necessarily the wrong approach." He looked to see if Laurie agreed. He seemed to want to say more, but strong emotion rendered him mute.

"You are the house surgeon at Queen Elizabeth Hospital for Children?"

"Yes."

"How many casualties did you receive on the night of the third of March?"

"Twenty-six altogether."

"How many living?"

"Twelve."

"And fourteen dead."

"Yes."

"Can you tell me the time of admission?"

"None of us seems to have noticed the exact time. I have the times when we wrote up the morphia for the living, and the first one was at ten past ten."

"What were the injuries to the living ones?"

"They were mostly bruised and shocked, very shocked. We had several of them x-rayed the next day and found no fractures."

"Right."

"It surprised me."

"I have no doubt. Did the dead bodies show similar injuries?"

"There were very few injuries on the dead ones."

"What was the cause of death—could you determine?"

"The first ones that came in, we did not know what had happened. We could not think why they were dead; they just seemed to have suffocated for no apparent cause."

"Blue appearance?"

"Yes. Unconsciousness among the victims on the stairs would have set in quickly, perhaps within twenty seconds, and death fifteen or twenty seconds after that."

Laurie frowned. This seemed to him reassuringly inaccurate. "Tell me," he asked, "isn't it possible for a person to hold his breath that amount of time?"

He decided to test the premise. Holding up his pocket watch, he drew a breath. The room, quiet already, grew quieter, pricking Laurie's ears. Outside they could hear a few people keeping up the familiar refrain ("The light"); a bird called; then the bells of St. John's marked noon. When the test was complete, Laurie blew out his breath and put the watch down. He raised his eyebrows.

The surgeon blushed and said that the time to death depended on the particular mechanism of asphyxia. "These victims suffered sudden compressive asphyxia. You may draw a large breath and hold it for sixty seconds, but the victims would not have had that advantage."

"No, of course not."

"Asphyxia causes generalized hypoxia, which is a pathological condition in which the body is deprived of an adequate oxygen supply. I can assure you that in cases of severe hypoxia, or hypoxia of very rapid onset, changes in levels of consciousness—seizures, coma, and death—occur quickly."

"I see," Laurie said. She was an intelligent woman. He didn't know why he'd put her on the spot. "Now, the survivors. How did some survive?"

She touched the curls at her neck. "Uneven weight distribution and oxygen pockets, I imagine." She was still upset. "Asphyxia is characterized by air hunger. The urge to breathe is actually triggered by rising carbon dioxide levels in the blood, not diminished oxygen levels. Depending on a person's concentration of red blood cells, air hunger will be more or less pronounced. Some of the victims, sustained by a small supply of oxygen, were able to exist in a state of mild hypoxia until the pressure abated."

Laurie nodded, hoping to show she'd satisfied the point. "And it surprised you that there were no broken bones."

"Yes, at first."

"But not now?"

"No."

"Why not?"

"I believe the crowd was never violent."

"But the pressure was relentless."

"Yes."

"And there is nothing else that strikes you, from what you have seen, that you would like to tell me?"

"No, I don't think so."

"Nothing of a peculiar nature?"

"No."

They called next a Dr. Woon, the doctor who had been one of the first on the scene outside the entrance. He'd been in the papers several times, always the same two details mentioned: that he was black or Asiatic but had done a lot of good. Now Laurie saw that he was a short, unsmiling Asiatic.

"At first the people didn't want me to touch them," Woon said, "but a nurse who was there told them I was a doctor, and then they allowed it."

"How did she know you were a doctor?"

"I assume she saw that I knew what I was doing."

"Of course."

"I treated a number of cases of shock. Quite a few cataleptic reactions."

"Cataleptic reactions?"

"A state of mental paralysis brought on by acute fear. The person is apathetic, cannot talk or move, looks like a dead man. Only the frightened eyes are alive. It can be quite disturbing to bystanders."

"I can imagine. What other injuries did you see?"

"Crushed kidneys. Burst lungs. A few cases of mild cerebral hypoxia."

"And what are the symptoms of that?"

"Confusion, decreased motor control, fainting, cyanosis."

"Cyanosis?"

"A blue discoloration of the skin."

"I see. And could that be confused in any way with the signs of a gas attack?"

"No."

"Are the symptoms of mild hypoxia reversible?"

"Usually."

"This has been very helpful, Dr. Woon. May I ask, why didn't you come forward sooner?"

"I did. The authorities at that time weren't interested."

"I see. I'm sorry."

Dr. Woon shrugged.

That evening the reporters caught Laurie on his way home. They asked about the first two days of testimony.

"I am very tired," was all he said, and this was printed in all the evening editions.

Twenty-four

Some people stayed in Bethnal Green, some went away, some went away and came back again. Not everyone who wanted to leave could, of course. But it was also true that not everyone who wanted to stay was suited to the new life. The difficulty of living in a place after a disaster is frequently underestimated. Attendance at the pubs went up, even on nights of a raid. How could the bombers pinpoint the pubs, as the early war propaganda said? The German pilots couldn't even find St. Paul's. So Bethnal Greeners, many of them, gathered and drank. In the bookshops, Bibles sold out as fast as publishers—limited by the paper shortage—could supply them. Evidence, some said, that people were looking for help. Proof, according to others, that faith can overcome the market.

St. John's had few Bibles, so Rev. McNeely referred the people who came looking for one to the Book of Common Prayer, several in every pew. He always took care to point out the complete Psalter within the BCP, but the people looked as if they were being asked to consider what they wanted in a different colour. They tilted their heads this way and that as if thinking about whether it would match what they already had. And they wanted to know if, like the soldiers at the front with their Penguin paperbacks, they might rip out that section and pass it along. Just until a complete Bible was found?

The people seemed to pity McNeely. A church without Bibles was another hardship of war, they thought, like the dearth of oranges and hairpins. But, as far as McNeely knew, the church had never had Bibles for browsing. If you had one in church, you had generally brought it yourself.

In the days after the accident, McNeely gave away twenty-three prayer books and three hymnals and vowed after the war to make a change: in his church there would be a Bible in every pew. Why not? Perhaps in the Church of England's noble effort to clarify the mysteries of the service, the comfort in the original source had been overlooked.

He kept the church open constantly, desperate to make it a haven, not because of, but rather in spite of, its proximity to the disaster. If he did not succeed, he worried the place would become a carcases, a hollow vault guilty for its failure to intervene. This was not rational, of course. How could a building prevent a tragedy? And yet how could the crush have happened in the shadow of a church? His church. Oh, why had the diocese sent him to Bethnal Green? His background was rural and his degree second-rate! He prayed for courage.

McNeely stood before the altar many evenings, great bunches of rosy willow herb absorbing his sneezes. He was allergic to the flower, but, as it grew well on bomb sites, along with yarrow, buddleia, and Oxford ragwort, the flower arrangers used little else. Later in the summer the bouquets were pretty, tall and graceful, but he looked forward to the end of the ban on flower transport. He hoped the flower arrangers did, too, and did not become attached to what they had begun to call the church's wartime look.

After the midday service on Wednesday, McNeely swept the nave. Two dozen parishioners had attended the ceremony, not bad for Lent, a difficult season in war. He took off his robe and reached for the roll he kept at the back of the shelf in the sacristy. He kept bread and other emergency refreshments stashed in various places around the church. After a few bites and a bit of water from a thermos, he felt better and resumed his post-service duties. At the altar he took the cup of leftover Eucharist wine and headed out to the garden behind the church. There, in an evergreen bed along the back wall filled mostly with varieties of juniper and trimmed with bulbs that came up in early spring, the ashes of a longtime St. John's parishioner were scattered. In life she'd been a repentant alcoholic, but before she died Mary Casey Cole asked McNeely if he would, after every service, drench her ashes in the leftover wine. He promised, and every time he carried out the duty, he hoped that one day someone might sift his own ashes with sugar.

"There you go, Mary," he said, shaking the last drop of wine from the chalice. He turned and saw Bertram Lodge watching him.

"What was she after, then?" Bertram said. "The blood or the wine?"

McNeely smiled. "Ah, well." He didn't want to reveal Mary's secret. He held out his arm and guided Bertram to the back step of the church. The two sat down.

The responsibility of tending to a parish felled by such a large tragedy was beginning to overwhelm McNeely. How much easier it would be to stay mobile, he thought, like the priests who followed the rescue units, attending to people here and there, bomb by bomb. The injuries were horrific, the deaths gruesome, but at least everything was visible. His congregation seemed to be suffering more mysteriously.

"Is there anything you need?" McNeely asked.

"Bertram Lodge," Bertram said, and put out his hand.

"I know. We've met before, Bertram."

"May I call you Lewis?"

"Of course. You have before."

Bertram thought a moment. "No. I don't think I can. But nice of you to say so, Reverend."

McNeely noticed that the boy's nails were chewed to the quick; his hair was so unwashed, it looked damp. He looked away to consider another approach, but his gaze fell on a bird. These sad little mounds, wings neatly folded, heads back, were not uncommon since clear glass had replaced the blown-out stained glass in the transept. The birds flew into the reflected trees and usually died instantly. This one must have been dead awhile. Ants, not legions, but enough, were swarming the eyes, forcing him to think they must be sweet.

"I'd like to ask you something," Bertram began.

"All right."

"Do you think He was there?"

McNeely waited, silently asking God to gather this boy to him.

"If it had been the church, the old crypt, that everyone was trying to get into? Would He have been there?"

"Oh, Bert. I don't think the place would have made a difference. We have to believe God always tries to be with us."

Bertram smiled. "No. He has requirements." He rubbed his hands together. "I'm so sorry I pushed. I know I did before I had to."

McNeely didn't know what to say.

Bertram pulled a piece of paper out of his pocket. On it was a short note in a woman's handwriting and, at the bottom, a fairly good portrait of Bertram. *I won't lose you,* the note said.

"She's worried about me," Bertram explained.

"I see."

Bertram sighed. "I'm afraid I don't believe in God. I hope that doesn't hurt your feelings. I didn't before the accident, either."

"God isn't supposed to test us, Bertram. At least, not more than we can stand." He didn't say that in Bertram's case, he wondered what He was doing.

McNeely was about to suggest that a special service, perhaps the Reconciliation of a Penitent, might be of use, but just then Bertram noticed the dead bird. He put the notebook down very gently. Then he scooped up the little bird with his hands. He carried the bird to the back of the garden, and, just about exactly where McNeely had given Mary a drink, he set the body down.

"Did she like birds?" he called.

"I don't know," McNeely said.

Bertram turned and walked back, his arms held out awkwardly at his sides.

"Would you like to wash your hands?" McNeely asked.

Twenty-five

Despite all Bertram's signs at the town hall and the hospitals, a few packages of clothes and personal items remained. Bertram blamed grief and confusion, but Clare said she believed there was a growing sense of guilt associated with the tragedy. People were trying to disassociate themselves from it. "That's why they haven't claimed the packages," she said.

"Then what are we doing?" Bertram asked. They'd left the flat together to deliver several of them.

"Your job. You need to finish this. The families will be grateful, too, whether they know it now or not."

The morning was cold, the sun in the wrong place in the sky, or so it seemed to Bertram. It kept surprising him around buildings and between trees, blinding him. Pigeons perched on the sunny corners of buildings, heads drawn down until they shook off the night freeze. Bertram saw a bald man who looked cold, worried. Everyone knew the clear sky meant the raids were likely to resume. The sight of the shiny scalp made Bertram involuntarily tap his own head, but Clare pulled his hand down.

The items they carried had belonged to a blond boy. His clothes were mended, his hair was recently trimmed, Bertram recalled. He could remember too well some of the bodies he'd seen. This boy's pockets had revealed an ink-bottle cork, a belt buckle, six beads from a necklace, and a ticket from the Museum Cinema.

The address was on a corner, the bottom flat of a three-storey terraced house. Bertram lost confidence at the gate, but

Clare pushed him through. A man answered quickly, and when Bertram didn't speak up, Clare said who they were, why they'd come. The man did not stoop or wilt. He just stood in the doorway, very still. Clare gave him a moment, wiping at the tip of her nose with the back of her mitten, then told him again what they'd brought. Sometimes a stillness like his means you aren't being believed, she'd told Bertram. But what Bertram had observed was the opposite: families who not only believed him but wanted to know more, who had opened their doors and let him in, as if on the other side of disaster there was a return to compassion.

"Please come in," the man in the doorway said, his voice a whisper.

The house smelled of the end of a meal. Bertram identified fried potatoes and bacon, a burned egg. The parents hastily folded up their bed, giving them all room to sit in the lounge. The mother put on a kettle. While they waited for the tea, the father fetched the boy's sister from the bedroom (the mother said "their bedroom", then shook her head but did not correct herself). Bertram, turning to Clare for direction, saw a tautness around her lips he didn't remember.

"We're so sorry," she said.

Bertram nodded. He looked at each of the people in the room—the boy's mother, bringing the tea tray; the tall father; the sleepy little sister still in her nightgown. Suddenly Bertram fumbled in his coat and took out the parcel he'd wrapped in a sheet of newspaper. It might have been fish-and-chips at another time, in another world. He dropped it on the table next to the teapot.

The mother opened the package quickly. The father switched on the lamp, casting an anxious increase of electric light into the already sunlit room. The mother pushed the tea out of the way and spread the items on the table, patting each one gently with her hands. She rearranged them, her hands beginning to shake. She rearranged them again, her expression changing, emotions moving across her face as though she were conversing, pleading, with the objects. Suddenly she stopped. She looked at the little girl, who, being seen, stepped sideways and grabbed her father's leg. With tremendous effort, the mother put her hands down on the table, lowered her forehead against them, and was still.

The little sister stepped forward and looked more closely at the beads.

"Would you like something to eat?" the father said, his voice hoarse.

"We never should have let them go alone," the mother said.

The father looked at Clare and Bertram. "He went to a film that night," he explained. "With a girl."

Bertram looked from the man to the woman and remembered the green-soled shoes. But that girl had not been with this boy. "I was there," he said.

The mother lifted her head. "Did you see him?"

There was so much hope in her eyes. Bertram thought it might stay there if he lied. "I'm not sure," he said. "I think so."

Clare looked at him.

"Why don't you—" the mother began.

"Lila, please," the father said. "What will it do?"

"I'm sorry," Clare said. "We have to go. We're so sorry about your son."

Outside, Bertram wrapped his arms around Clare before she could say anything. It was all he knew how to do, and she'd told him once he was good at it. She pushed him away. "I know you were trying to help them, but you can't. Not like that."

He nodded.

They stopped briefly in St. John's. Clare knelt in a back pew; Bertram sat. Up by the altar he could see Rev. McNeely sweeping. Bertram waved, then glanced at his watch, hoping it was time for the bells. Then he remembered there were no church bells anymore, just as there were no weather reports, no lights at night, no flowers. London was desperate, and he felt so sorry for the streets and buildings, for the people scurrying along them, that a few minutes later, leaving the church with Clare, he clutched his stomach, doubled over, and vomited into the gutter.

Clare rubbed his back until he was finished. "Let's get you home," she said.

Twenty-six

"You say you noticed that the Museum Cinema up the street was turning out and people were dashing into the street. Were they worried?"

"No."

"Jumpy?"

"No, just heading for shelter, I think. On that occasion the picture palace seemed to empty all at once."

"It was not closing time or anything like that?"

"No."

"Do you think they'd heard the siren and they thought they would be safer somewhere else?"

"Yes."

"It is a biggish cinema?"

"A fair-sized picture palace, sir."

"And you say the people were coming out quickly?"

"Some of them. Not running, though. Nothing like that."

"Did you see the constable at the entrance?"

"No, sir."

"You were already in the shelter? You had got down there, had you?"

"Yes."

"Did you pass a constable on your way in?"

"No, sir."

"Could you see over the heap of people on the stairs?"

"No, sir."

"Were there people on the landing between the flights of steps?"

"One or two."

"Fallen bodies?"

"No, these were people on their legs."

"I am trying to see what happened. There was no one on the landing?"

"No, sir. Just a wall of people stretched the whole way across the bottom step."

"And how long do you think this wall received additions to it? How long did the pressure go on?"

"Well, that is hard to say, but a short time."

"A short time?"

"Maybe a matter of seconds."

"When you got to the shelter, what was happening?"

"There was a crowd."

"Was there a constable at the entrance?"

"No, sir."

"Did you see or hear anything unusual?"

"I saw some lights dropping from the sky, sir. I don't know what they were. When I got to the fourth stair, something large and heavy went off."

"You mean a sound of some kind?"

"Yes."

"We just need your help a little bit more here, officer. Thank you for coming back. I'd like to know the farthest point of Constable Henderson's patrol from the shelter."

"Well, it extends from Cambridge Heath Railway Station to Mile End Gate, the shelter being approximately mid-way."

"So the farthest point?"

"Couldn't be more than a quarter mile."

"No more than five minutes, then?"

"That's what I would think."

"But he does not seem to have got to the shelter until the trouble had already started. And we know that was at least ten minutes after the alert."

"Yes, sir."

"Have you been into this with him at all?"

"He says it took him four minutes from the time of the alert, which I am satisfied is an understatement."

"An understatement?"

"Yes."

"So you are investigating this?"

"Not at this time."

"You were at the shelter, were you, on this particular night?"

"No, sir."

"You did not go there at all?"

"I've said nothing about that."

Laurie looked at Ross, then back at the witness. "I'm sorry, you did not go there at all?"

"Yes, sir, I lost two children. I searched among the dead for them."

"That is awful."

"They're all right now."

"They're all right?"

"Yes, they came through."

"Did you go with them to the shelter that night?"

"Yes, sir, with the wife and children. We were nine in all."

"Let us start from the beginning."

In the afternoon Laurie noticed a grey moth hiding on one of the upholstered chairs. The moth had oriented itself so as to fit in with the upholstery design, an impressive bit of camouflaging, although the insect couldn't help its colour. When Ross returned from lunch, Laurie pointed out the moth. It seemed to him a sign they would uncover something soon, but Ross just stared, baffled.

Laurie looked down at the name on his paper. "Bertram Lodge?"

Ross held the door, and the pale clerk bobbed in. He had a white parting in his hair like a gash and put himself in the chair as if trying to collect his bones into the smallest possible pile.

"You've been unwell?" Laurie asked.

The rims of Bertram's eyes reddened a shade. His skin looked sensitive, almost damp. Despite his pathetic manner, however, he seemed to show a certain disdain for the proceedings by wearing, Laurie was fairly certain, his pyjama top under a cardigan and a pair of mismatched boots.

"These chairs," Laurie said, looking about the room. "You placed them, correct? They have not been unuseful."

"Thank you, sir."

"They did some good, actually. Got the government to release the number of dead sooner."

"One hundred and seventy-three," Bertram said. "Five fewer than previously feared." He eyed a few chairs as if he thought he might immediately remove them for acuracy's sake. "Sixty-one injured."

"Right." Laurie looked at his notes. "Let's begin. When you arrived at the shelter on the third of March, what did you see?"

"The entrance backed up with people."

"What were they doing?"

"Pushing."

Laurie looked at him. "Pushing."

"Yes."

Laurie looked at Ross, then down at his papers.

"Mr. Lodge, you are the first person to come before this inquiry and say there was pushing."

The boy looked confused. "If others don't feel guilty—"

"I don't know about that. Perhaps they describe it differently. Why was there pushing, then?" Laurie asked.

"Something seemed to be wrong. The crowd wasn't moving." Bertram let a degree of rudeness that astonished him into his voice.

"Was there a constable at the entrance?"

"One or two."

"What were they doing?"

"Trying to clear some of the people away. After a while, they advised us to go to another shelter. Some people did."

"Did these constables use force at all?"

"Yes, sir."

"But only in the sense of dragging people away?"

"Yes, that's right."

Laurie nodded. "Now, Mr. Lodge, I'd like to ask you about your correspondence with the Regional Commissioners—"

"It wasn't mine. I just sent the letters back and forth, back and forth."

Laurie kneaded the back of his neck. "Right. Well, maybe you could elaborate a little for me. What exactly is missing?"

"Several letters and a plan."

"A plan?"

"A plan. A drawing. The local council had an engineer draw up a plan to change the entrance because they were worried about a crush. I sent it to the Regional Commissioners for approval."

"When was this?"

"Nineteen forty-one. Between September and November. By about Christmas we gave up."

"This correspondence should have been in this building, the town hall?"

"Yes."

"Do you have any idea why it isn't?"

"I imagine it has something to do with the Regional Commissioners' refusal to permit the work."

"And what reason did they give?"

"Waste of money."

Laurie shook his head, the lines across his forehead twitching in consternation. Bertram cracked the knuckles of one hand and asked if the interview was over. Laurie nodded.

"Then may I show you something, sir?" Bertram reached into the bag at his feet. "Mr. Wycomb says the Regional Commissioners requested this, but now the Regional Commissioners say they did not. They think it was the London County Council or possibly the Ministry of Information." He opened the notebook as he spoke. "I was asked to inventory the victims' belongings. The bodies were still in the hospital and the morgue, and I went through their pockets, but now no one seems to want the list. No one seems to know who needed it."

"Let me see," Laurie said. He skimmed a few pages, read what he might have expected:

Amanda Park: four buttons, a hairpin, some crushed juniper needles
Paul Popper: one white chess bishop, a pair of steel pocket scissors
Eliza Cannon: a reel of blue thread, a buttonhook, a small pocket
    handkerchief monogrammed WFW, a trunk key
William Fendell: nine pennies, a toothpick, a key ring

Not one of the casualties had more than half a dozen items, Bertram said. The children, in general, had nothing but small toys and scraps, sometimes one or two boiled sweets. One elderly man had a silver pocket watch that looked to be valuable. The women seemed united in their possession of cottonreels, probably intending to get the mending done until they could sleep.

Laurie closed the notebook.

"Looking at the still bodies was the hardest part," Bertram said. "After I got used to it, touching was less difficult than I thought it would be. I tried to be gentle, but some of the pockets were so small. I had to apologize to a little boy whose only possession was a key on a strip of leather."

Laurie cleared his throat. "Did you return the items to the families?" he asked quietly.

Bertram explained that most of the families had seen his signs and claimed the items at the town hall. His girlfriend had arranged for the mobile canteen to serve tea. The unclaimed items, he'd wrapped in paper and distributed personally.

"Good." Laurie held the notebook out to Bertram.

Ross stood, but Bertram didn't move.

"Sir, I'm not an expert, but I wanted to say that I agree with the coroner's evidence. The victims did not look like there'd been a stampede or a panic. Blood was only in their mouths, sir. No twisted limbs. Very bad bruising, of course, but that's to be expected.

"I saw all the bodies, sir, eighty-four women, sixty-two children, twenty-seven men."

"You've done a good job," Laurie said. "It must have been very difficult."

Bertram took the notebook. "What am I to do with it?"

All three men stared at the green cover. "Type it up," Laurie said. "I believe it can be said someone will want it eventually."

Bertram asked if it should be alphabetized.

"I don't see how that will matter much."

"Plain or bond paper?" Bertram asked.

Laurie turned to Ross.

"All right, Bert," Ross said. "Time to go."

When Constable Henderson reappeared, he was nervous and slightly drunk. He announced that he was off duty but that, as he had an academic interest in history, he was more than happy to see them again. Ross smiled.

"Very kind," Laurie said. "An academic interest, you say?"

"Yes, sir, though I don't have time right now to indulge it."

"So that's not why you weren't at the entrance when you should have been the night of the third of March? You weren't studying your history books?"

Henderson turned red.

"I don't mind telling you that I and several of your superior officers believe there are some miscalculations in your statement about when you arrived at the entrance."

"Yes, sir."

"Do you have anything to add? Would you like to revise your statement?"

"I stopped, sir, for a few minutes." He rubbed his face as if to banish the beer. "There was a group of boys with torches they weren't handling properly. They were running and waving 'em, sir. I thought someone might get hit, you know. They also had a couple of bottle rockets."

"Bottle rockets?"

"Yes. Three or four, I think."

"Did they set these off?"

"Not while I was there."

"If they had set some off earlier, before you came upon them, could someone have mistaken the sound for that of bombs or anti-aircraft fire?"

"Hard to imagine, sir."

"Why is that?"

"Everyone knows what a bottle rocket sounds like, don't they?"

"Were the boys shouting anything?"

"No."

"Not inciting the crowd in any way?"

"No, sir. Just running around with their torches." He shook his head slowly. "Sir, if I'd known that something was going to happen at the shelter, I would have ignored those boys and walked right on as fast as I could. But on another night, I might have been reprimanded for not speaking to them." Henderson put his hand over his eyes. "It's hard, sir, to know what's right."

Laurie conceded that that was certainly true.

Twenty-seven

They ate their cake quickly, Laurie pleased with both it and the progress of the interview. He was glad he'd bought the cake, even though it had taken him several minutes of deliberation in the shop. After the war, the habit of deciding when such a treat was justified lasted a lifetime. He'd revised, however, his opinion on the merits of a casual luncheon, thought he might even consider eating outside next time if the weather were cooler. He'd tell the mighty William that the younger members of the club were on to something after all.

He enjoyed Barber, found him clever and appreciative of the report. It touched him when the boy had shown up for their second interview wearing a tie. At least that was what Laurie thought it was, though it was as wide as a plank.

But talking to him was like talking to any young person about the war years: they spoke from a background of black-and-white pictures, while your memories were very much in colour. They asked about the rationing, while you saw coupons. They spoke about the public morale, when what you remembered were the faces. Try as they might, they heard only a chord or two, while the whole symphony still roared in your head. Laurie felt he was back in the house on Bonner Road again, with Armorel, sirens wailing. He had that old peculiar feeling of waiting for the planes rushing towards them in the dark.

And yet it was a relief to be discussing Bethnal Green again. He disagreed with the view, expressed in a number of articles over the years, that he'd done little else of consequence. He thought he'd shown courage in his handling of a number of extradition and deportation cases after the war, but opinion had swung against him. Before the war the public praised his ability to resist extralegal pressure. After the war his judgements were considered insensitive. He'd been told he did not understand the difficulties of the era.

Bollocks.

Barber was saying something about the plight of messengers.

Laurie sighed and wondered aloud if Samuel Johnson would have agreed that, like second marriage, producing a report was the triumph of hope over experience. He was eager to turn the conversation to lighter topics. The day demanded it. But Barber had opened his notebook and was studying a page.

"A refugee?" Barber said. "The first woman who fell? But wouldn't that suggest—"

"Is a mistake always an accident? An accident always a mistake?" Laurie said. He closed his eyes and rubbed his face. The wine was making him glib. He'd never been able to drink quite as much as his friends and remain discreet.

"Low committed suicide," he said suddenly, rubbing the back of his neck. "The chief warden of the shelter."

Barber stared.

"There. Something new. That's what you want, isn't it? He tried to resign. Sent a letter to the home secretary, but we wouldn't accept it. *I* wouldn't accept it."

"That's not in the report."

"Right."

"Why not?"

"Someone stepping forward to accept responsibility doesn't do away with the need for blame."

"Doesn't it depend on who the person is?"

"Does it? In my experience what people want to believe is more important to them than what actually happens."

Then Laurie, forgetting he was not, in fact, in Bonner Road, reached for the lamp that would have been on the table next to the chair. But that table had not been moved to the house in Nelson Close, and the room wasn't really dark yet. His hand groped a moment, then sank. Barber seemed not to have noticed, but Laurie covered it with a few coughs and a stretch.

Barber said, "You didn't assign individual blame."

"It's a relief to know that hasn't been forgotten. It wouldn't have been fair to her."

"Who?"

"Ada Barber."

Twenty-eight

It was obvious Ada had taken great care with her clothes, her best grey wool, a blue scarf over her hair. She had long legs, a round middle, and pitched herself forwards when she walked, like a shorebird. Ross was standing when she came in, so she sat in one of the wooden chairs and wouldn't move when Laurie indicated that she might be more comfortable in the armchair. She was very nervous. Ross made a cup of tea; Laurie closed the window.

"How are you feeling?"

"A little better. I'm still very shaky."

"It is Ada Barber?"

"Yes."

"Three Jersey Street, Bethnal Green?"

"Yes, sir."

"On the third of March, you went to the air-raid shelter with your daughters?"

"Yes, sir."

"How long after the warning did you get there?"

"Soon after the warning left off."

"How far is it from your home?"

"I should think it would take us five or six minutes."

"There were a number of people hurrying along, too? Like you?"

"Yes."

"What did you do?"

"I was going down the stairs, as usual, when there was a rush behind me. I was holding on to my two girls, and as I went down the rush dragged me along the wall. I got to the bottom, and a man pulled us out, on the right side, where there was a lane open for a moment. We were the last ones out before the accident." Ada's voice had started strong but now thinned to a whisper. "Have you talked to him?"

"Who?"

"The man at the bottom of the stairs."

"What's his name?"

"I don't know. I just wonder, have you talked to anyone who said they helped out a woman and her girl before the crush?"

"In general, Mrs. Barber, I am here to ask you questions, but I can tell you that no one's told us yet that they were able to pull anyone out."

Ada readjusted herself on the chair.

"You said a lane was open for a moment?"

"Yes."

"How, exactly?"

Ada swallowed. "A woman fell."

"Yes," Laurie said, "I've heard that. Do you know who she was?"

"No."

Something made Laurie wait.

"I only knew her name. Mrs. W."

"Mrs. W.?"

"Mrs. Wigdorowicz. We shortened it, everyone shortened it."

"Mrs. W. Mrs. Four-by-Two," Ross whispered to Laurie, illustrating for him the rhyming slang.

"I see," Laurie said.

"She tripped," Ada said. "It was awful. But I had my girls with me, so I had to keep moving." She tucked her hands beneath her legs, trying to warm them between wool and wood.

"Perhaps you knew her a little from the area?"

"She came into our shop sometimes, but they don't make a regular practice of it. They shop around, sometimes as far as Stepney."

"They? The Jewish refugees?"

"Yes."

"How did she trip?"

"She was carrying something, a load of blankets and pillows. It was too much for her." Her voice had been fast and bright. Now it went flat. "And some people say a baby. I didn't know it at the time."

"Did the infant survive?"

"I don't know."

"And this was on the right-hand side of the stairway?"

"Yes. The crowd was packed but on the move."

"And the force swept you through to the other end?"

Ada nodded. "I have been going down to the shelter since the beginning and never take anything. I'm always careful."

"Have you ever had any trouble before?"

"No."

"What do you think of the entrance?"

"It is very dark."

"But you have always got up and down all right?"

"Yes."

"You have not known many people to tumble on the stairs?"

"No. And there wouldn't have been any trouble this night if that first woman had stayed on her feet."

"Did you see her fall?"

"It's hazy now."

"Of course. What do you remember?"

Ada hugged herself and rubbed her sleeves. "I don't know. The stairwell was so dark; everyone was hurrying." She began to rock and looked up suddenly. "I lost one of my girls, Mr. Dunne."

"I'm so sorry. Mrs. Barber, it is our hope—"

"Too late for that!"

"Your surviving child. She was pulled out by this man you mentioned?"

"Tilly," Ada said. "Emma is the one I lost."

Laurie turned to Ross, who quickly produced a handkerchief.

"Would Tilly speak to us?" Ross asked.

"No," she said. She looked scared.

Laurie frowned. He'd interviewed few children, finding them unreliable at best, but Ada's reaction interested him.

"Why?"

"She hasn't talked since the accident."

"It's a common reaction. I might be able to reassure her."

"Could I stay with her?" Ada asked. "I wouldn't want her to tell any stories."

So is the girl mute or a liar? Laurie wondered. He told Ada she could remain when Tilly came.

At the door Ada turned around. "I remembered something. Mrs. Wigdorowicz's name was Raisa." She paused.

"I'll make a note of it," Laurie said.

"It means 'rose'."

On 14 March, a Sunday, the inquiry did not meet. "Because the story should add up to more than the facts," Laurie told Ross. "That's faith, and our report is going to need it."

But the sermon at St. James's that day irritated and annoyed him. Concerned with the hierarchy of angels, it seemed more than unusually irrelevant. After the service he and Armorel walked back to No. 17 Bonner Road. The row of fine eighteenth-century houses had not been directly hit, but the street was suffering a slow dilapidation and looked shabby in the sunlight. Half the residents had gone to weather the war elsewhere; those who remained were understandably negligent. Only the Dunnes' house, with its ruddy brown brick and painted red door, still had a winter wreath in place. Seeing it, Laurie took Armorel's hand.

"It looks nice, doesn't it?" she said.

After lunch, Laurie worked and Armorel read. He'd been listening to nothing but Bach since the inquiry started, mostly the Goldberg Variations but also the cello suites. The structure of these monumental works calmed the agitation he felt about the inquiry.

"What about a little Mozart?" Armorel asked when she joined him in the study with her tea and a book. "Wouldn't that help?"

"No." After a moment he relented and asked what she was reading.

"*Wife to Mr. Milton,*" Armorel said, "by Robert Graves." She turned the book over in her hand and examined the cover. "I thought it was going to be a biography, but it appears to be a novel about the life of Milton's first wife."

"Any good?"

"Very. Better, probably."

In the late afternoon they went for a walk in Victoria Park and stood for a time on the bridge over the narrow end of the lake. Laurie said he was enjoying the Taverner and was eager to try some new flies in Scotland.

"When will we go?" Armorel asked.

"Oh, not until the inquiry's over. And then, once the report is published, I'll need to be in London, I should think. Autumn, probably."

"Good. I don't want to leave Elizabeth at the moment."

"How is she?"

"Not well, but I've got her working again on the landscape. She's quite good, and the RAF is eager for it."

He patted his wife's shoulder.

"You're wrong, you know," she said. "From fifty feet up they give an accurate impression of what the landscape will look like from the cockpit."

"But how? Where do they do this?"

"Hertfordshire. An airplane hanger there, apparently. They

put all the quilts together, and the pilots study them from scaffolding up to the ceiling. They told us there's been a decrease in the amount of creep-back when the pilots have practised with a landscape beforehand." She pronounced "creep-back" with the solemnity befitting its new place in the language. The phenomenon—successive waves of bombers retreating from a target—was a national curiosity.

"I'm surprised it's not Lord's," he said. "Or Wembley. Sounds like sport. Probably will be after the war."

Armorel didn't smile. Her expression told him that she'd moved on to something else. "I've done some research for you."

"Oh?"

Armorel stopped walking. "How wide are the stairs at Bethnal Green?"

"Ten feet."

"And how many handrails are there?"

"Handrails down both sides. Why?"

"When were they put in?"

"I assume they've been there since the beginning of the war."

"Do you know how many staircases in London have a centre rail?" She waited, but he didn't have an answer. "All of them that are that wide. Except Bethnal Green."

He looked at her. "What are you up to? Examining the staircases of London?"

She took his hand and smiled. "I can't help it. I need to know what happened."

He nodded, and they walked in silence for a while.

"I read in the *Evening News* that mothers were found crouched over their babies."

He shook his head. "It took them three hours to remove the bodies, Armorel. The positions were countless, I'm sure."

"No. You look into it. You'll find those were the babies who were safe."

At home a messenger was waiting for him with a note from Morrison: *Received a resignation yesterday from James Low. Seems he's responsible for no light on the stairs. Says this caused the crush. The letter is dated 4 March, but I've only just seen it. I'll await word from you before releasing the news and taking the appropriate steps.*

For several hours Laurie sat in his study and read through his notes. The accident was a mystery. He'd thought at first that the stories wouldn't hold up to scrutiny, but the coroner confirmed almost everything: some people at the bottom survived, while people on top did not. The coroner recorded changes in the victims' blood caused by suffocation, and stomachs and intestines distended to a gross degree. In the injured the pathologist noted shock, concussion, and severe bruising in the muscle tissues, contusions of a kind usually associated with pinning by collapsed houses or other heavy debris. And yet there was only one fracture, a fibula, and this in a five-year-old girl at the very bottom— almost the last to be rescued—who got up and limped away by herself.

Mrs. Barber's testimony was odd but hardly noteworthy. In his experience women like her often pointlessly distrusted authority. He hadn't been able to locate any record of a Mrs. Wigdorowicz in the area and so couldn't confirm if she was the first woman to fall. Constable Henderson undoubtedly should have reached the shelter entrance sooner and, in doing so, might have done some good. But would he have prevented the crush? Probably not. If Warden Low knew his constituency as well as he said, then perhaps he should not have increased the wattage of the stairway bulb. Was this the cause of the accident? Hardly. What about the shelterers who smashed it? Should he track them down and punish them? Magistrates all over the city had been doing that since the war began, with no appreciable change. The manager of the Museum Cinema seemed to have insisted after the alert that the people leave. Should this man be responsible for contributing to the crush that night? Should the city now have a law that required cinema managers to keep their patrons in when there was a raid? Ridiculous.

Laurie had spoken to members of the local Home Guard and learned there was an experimental weapon in the battery in Victoria Park. It was one of the new rocket guns to be used soon in defence of the city. Could there have been a test that night? he'd asked. The Home Guard adamantly denied it. They had been told there would be a special warning before the first test. There had been no warning, therefore no test.

Frustrated, Laurie put off replying to Morrison's latest correspondence and settled down with his Taverner. Just before dinner, he came across this: *No one knows why a salmon takes a fly. We cannot tell whether the fish takes it because he recognizes something which he fed on in the sea; or because he is annoyed by something darting before him.*

The consequences of annoyance—this intrigued him. After all, who has felt the fullness of true rage? Not many, he thought. Mostly people move through life doing their best to calm the minor urges. It was worth remembering. Then, while he was eating leftover Woolton pie with Armorel, she spoke about the trouble she was having finding needles with which to work on the landscape and how frustrated she'd become with a shopkeeper who had sold out of the sudden small shipment he'd received by the time she got there.

"I actually slapped the counter," she confessed. "I can't believe it. And if a counter had not stood between us, I think I might have slapped him. It's just too troubling that the best needles are German."

"The least emotion," she said.

"What is?" he asked, surprised her thoughts aligned so well with his.

"Annoyance."

———

When Morrison had not heard from Laurie by the next morning, he rang. The two exchanged pleasantries, though Morrison called Armorel "Armora". Laurie reminded himself that Morrison was a man who would be, in all likelihood, principally remembered for giving his name to a steel coffee table, the Morrison shelter. Laurie put his foot on it while he spoke.

"The matter at Bethnal Green is not about a lightbulb," he said.

"No?"

"No. Did the night begin without a light? Or was it smashed by shelterers worried it was too bright? Either way, it doesn't matter."

Morrison had a habit of ticking his tongue when he was thinking, putting Laurie in mind of a field in summer.

"But I have a resignation."

"Low's popular. No one wants this."

"A resignation is only useful if it's been demanded?"

"In my experience."

"But if it's his fault?"

"It's not. His only crime might be expecting other people to do their best."

More ticking, then Laurie heard him send someone out of the room. Laurie thought about mentioning the woman who'd fallen but held back. "I'd like to know more about the new rocket guns," he said.

"Why?"

"I think the people heard something different on the third. Many have spoken about a strange sound, not the anti-aircraft fire they're used to."

More ticking, then silence. "The Home Guard were not called out on the third of March," Morrison said. "There was no anti-aircraft response that night because there were no planes."

"But the people heard—"

"The people panicked," Morrison interrupted.

"Why? What scared them? They've never panicked before. Something must have set the crowd off."

Morrison was quiet. Then he asked Laurie to ring him if he needed anything. "We're looking forward to the results of your inquiry."

But Laurie couldn't stop. "Almost everyone I know deplores it when the poor are mistreated or ignored, but it continues to happen. Why is that?"

Morrison sounded angry. "We knew all along these stations weren't ideal or even appropriate as shelters. The official policy is dispersal, as you well know. And yet the people wanted large shelters. Now that the unthinkable has happened—"

"But it wasn't unthinkable! One entrance to a shelter for ten thousand? They tried to get improvements to the entrance and were turned down, apparently."

"Mr. Dunne."

Laurie asked to be remembered to all the members of Morrison's family, every one of whom he named correctly, then put the phone down. He knew now for certain that he was being asked to investigate one thing while leaving something else entirely in the dark. He looked over at the Taverner, on his chair, and it occurred to him for the first time that he might not be able to complete a record of the Bethnal Green disaster that approached its depth and accuracy, an encyclopedia of fish.

Twenty-nine

When the baby came home with Ada, he was four months old, as near as anyone could tell. He was very good and quiet, quieter than either of Ada's girls had been at the same age. He had round, dark eyes, a beautiful mouth, and a wide-open belly button, a little crater, not the tight swirls of her daughters. Ada asked her midwife about it, and the midwife said it meant he wouldn't keep secrets.

"He won't have them, or he won't be able to?" Ada asked.

"He won't want to," the midwife replied.

But Ada worried that it somehow meant the twist and clamp of the cord had not completely severed the connection to his mother.

They made a bed for him in the drawer they'd used for the girls and kept him on the floor by the window. Every morning Ada washed him in a tub filled with warm water from several kettles. She'd forgotten just how busy life was with a baby, but Tilly was helping again, and Robby was managing the shop. Friends often stopped by with food. Mr. Levin from across the hall brought a loaf of bread and a small outfit wrapped in muslin that had been his as a child. He said he'd been away the night of the accident but had followed the aftermath closely. She was astonished. She had very few baby clothes and nothing for a boy, but why had he saved these precious things? Why weren't the little shirt and trousers with his mother? The questions felt too late for someone she'd been living across the hall from for years. And so they stood together, looking down at the sleeping baby in silence.

As word spread, other neighbours came by.

"He's sweet."

"You're kind."

"I wish I could help, but with my three still at home . . ."

Then one morning she went to the door, and the man who'd been at the bottom of the shelter stairs was there, the one who had helped her on the landing. He introduced himself. "Bill Steadman," he said softly, red in the face and out of breath. He held out a white baby blanket tied with a blue ribbon. She took it, thanked him, and closed the door. Everyone who had brought the baby something was either a friend or a neighbour, and she hadn't invited any of them in. Why should she treat him differently? Still, she froze, unable to walk away from the door, unwilling to let him know she was still there. She could hear him breathing, waiting. He cleared his throat.

"It's all right," he said. "You don't have to worry. I will never say anything."

Ada held her breath. She stayed balanced forwards on her toes so that the floorboard beneath her wouldn't squeak. When she heard his soles retreating in the gritty passage, she sank to her knees, her head against the door. Tilly found her there.

"Mum?"

Ada smiled and scrambled up. "Look what someone just brought!" she said.

"Who?"

Ada turned the blanket over, pretending to look for a card. "Oh, well. Just put it with the other things."

No one knew the baby's name. The other orphans were identified by relatives in the area who came forward with church records even if they couldn't adopt them. Mrs. Barton-Malow checked the register of births but couldn't find anything conclusive about this baby. His mother, she thought, must have given birth alone.

"You'll have to name him," Mrs. Barton-Malow said to Ada before she left the orphanage.

Ada shook her head. So much had been taken from this baby; she didn't want to take his name, too! She remembered Raisa as she'd looked the summer before, when she first started coming into Ada's shop. She wore long, shapeless dresses and must have already been pregnant. Once, maybe because it was summer, maybe because the morning sickness had passed and she was feeling better—who would ever know?—she had smiled at Ada and patted her stomach.

"Raisa," Mrs. W. said suddenly, moving her hand up to pat her chest.

"Ada."

Mrs. W. smiled. But what she said next, Ada didn't understand, and the woman's face turned anxious.

"Growing?" Mrs. W. said. "Growing. Garden?"

"No," Ada said, shaking her head.

Mrs. W. left quickly. Had she wanted Ada to know her name meant "rose"? Or was she telling her she was growing a baby? When Ada told Robby about it later, he said maybe Mrs. W. knew the English liked to garden.

After that, whenever she came into the shop, Ada tried to catch her eye, say hello, but Raisa had gone back to being quiet, almost furtive. Ada thought there might be something wrong with her. There was something hard about her eyes, something cold and faraway. Perhaps this made sense, given what she'd been through. But it had seemed to Ada that she would have tried harder.

Mrs. Barton-Malow was touching the baby's cheek. "What about Justin?" she said, and Ada was very surprised to see that she was crying.

"Did you know a Justin?"

Mrs. Barton-Malow nodded. "It's such a nice name."

When Ada got the baby home—after paying a series of fees to Mrs. Barton-Malow, all of which sounded official, most of which she didn't understand, and none of which she could have afforded without the money Tilly got from the reporter—she tried whispering names in his ear, sure that if she hit on the right one, or something close, she would see some kind of recognition. She went through all the Jewish names she could think of, then opened the Bible and started at the beginning. Nothing. Mostly he slept. She could rouse him by tickling his feet, but then he would just bring up some milk and frown.

After three days Ada called Rev. McNeely. He agreed to come but seemed uncomfortable and didn't want to name the baby.

"Why not?" Ada asked.

"Mum," Tilly warned, sitting on the floor, rocking the baby to sleep.

"Perhaps there's a male relative—" he tried.

Ada shook her head.

"Mum," Tilly said, hoping to help Rev. McNeely. "Didn't you have any boy's names picked out?"

"We would have named a boy for your father."

All three stared at the baby, who was nearly asleep.

"There is the story of Paul," McNeely offered.

Ada and Tilly waited.

"The apostle. He was Saul, a Jew, but when he became a Christian, he changed his name to Paul. After he fell off the horse."

He shook his head and blushed. It was an extremely inadequate retelling, but he didn't know how to fix it. He couldn't very well ask Ada not to baptize the boy, and yet he was astonished at how ambivalent he felt. But she was a grieving mother; he felt battered and wordless in her presence. The best thing to do, he thought, was give the boy a name from a story that reflected his heritage.

When Robby came home that evening, Ada had dinner almost

ready. She'd managed to buy a piece of fish, and not whale meat but cod. She paused in her cooking and looked through to the lounge. Tilly was reading. Paul was asleep in the basket. "Go and see your son," she said, and felt a subtle shift. Your son. Robby was confused by the turn their lives had taken—she knew that—but he didn't have the will to resist.

Thirty

"So, a copy of the plan the Bethnal Green local council sent to the Regional Commissioners for approval has turned up."

"Yes, sir."

"Just this morning. Quite remarkable. You are a member of the local council?"

"That is right."

"Well, the plan is here, which solves one mystery. But now we have another one. This plan does not actually address the problem of the entrance stairs."

"Sir—"

"A steep, often dark set of stairs. Did it not occur to the council that a rush of people might have trouble navigating them?"

"Of course. That was obvious, so—"

"So the plan was to strengthen the gate, a gate that could not have been closed against a large crowd. Is it not a matter of critical importance to consider the possibility of a rush by a crowd?"

"Yes, sir. I would agree. We were just following the advice of the borough engineer."

"You are the borough engineer to Bethnal Green Council?"

"Yes, sir."

"How long have you held that position?"

"About four years, sir."

"Could you tell me about the work you did for the local council?"

"Yes. It was on the minds of the local council and their staff that there might be trouble at the shelter entrance."

"What kind of trouble?"

"That crowds might come along and endeavour to gain access, and that when the gates were closed, the hoarding would not hold."

"And the region turned down the scheme you proposed?"

"Yes."

"And that plan—correct me if I'm mistaken—proposed strengthening the existing gates?"

"Yes, sir."

"The idea, then, generally, was to close those gates in the event of a rush?"

"Well, I think the idea was to close one gate at a time."

"Tell me, which way do the gates open?"

"Inwards, sir."

"Yes, inwards. So you thought, If a crowd comes along, we'll just close the gates until they calm down a bit?"

"With hindsight, sir, I see that with a very big crowd, you cannot close gates of that nature in a rush."

"But is that not exactly what you were asked to consider?"

"How long have you been a Regional Commissioner, Mr. Gowers?"

"Since the beginning of the war. May I just say before we really get started that I think undoubtedly the entrance to the Bethnal Green shelter should have been improved upon. But whether you can blame those who dealt with it—that is to say, the local authority or the Regional Commissioners—in the atmosphere of the time is difficult to say."

"I am not really concerned with blame."

"I understand. I used the wrong word."

"I am concerned with responsibility. If I say I'm going to give you a piece of fruit but hand you a vegetable, wouldn't you correct me? Or would you just hand it back and say, 'This is not a fruit'?"

"I'm afraid I don't follow."

"The local council proposed the wrong solution for the right problem, but all you did was refuse the plan. Why didn't you make a counterproposal? Why didn't you tour the site with a member of the local council and see what they were talking about?"

"You mean hand them an apple when they're holding a potato?"

"For God's sake."

"With hindsight, I wish we had."

Thirty-one

There was nowhere to go, no holiday to take, unless perhaps you walked to the old Weavers Fields, or went to the movies, or picked your way to the shipping docks along the Thames. Rain and steady funerals kept spirits low. A shop would be open one day, closed the next; no one knew why or when it would reopen. The problem was this: the people had girded themselves against the war, but they had trusted the shelters. After the disaster their confidence in everything was chilled.

Some in Bethnal Green were eager for the report, sure it would reveal something to help them make sense of the senseless. Others felt only suspicion. The inquiry, they believed, was merely an exercise in distraction, something authorities did in order to avoid accountability. How could someone not present that night tell them what had happened?

In general, though, tempers were beginning to cool. The influx of money had that effect. So astonishing was it to see improvements being made to the shelter entrance that many people forgot what it meant: if these changes could be authorized now, couldn't they have been authorized earlier? It was typical of government bureaucracy: repairs proceeded, no one ever admitting that repairs were necessary. New walls protecting the entrance, new lighting, new handrails down the sides and center. Everything was shiny, well made, and well installed. The money came from the borough council and several anonymous donors from the West End.

———

McNeely's parish adamantly refused the government's offer of a mass funeral. But he suspected they'd embrace a memorial service held on the two-week anniversary of the event. He considered an all-night vigil, but memories of the poorly attended overnight watch during Holy Week last year persuaded him against it. "Can you not stay awake with me one hour?"—Christ's words to his disciples in the garden of Gethsemane—had not compelled his flock as much as he'd hoped. Better to plan a short service, then perhaps a march. He'd get them on their feet, move them through the streets again so that they could regain their confidence. He checked with the air-raid protection officials, who insisted that—the powerful communal grief notwithstanding—he could not walk through the streets at night with candles. If he wanted to distribute candles, he'd have to hold the service earlier. Even then, the officials told him not to exceed one candle per ten demonstrators.

He made signs and put them up all over the neighbourhood. He took out a small ad in the *Observer*, which by chance appeared the same day the coroner announced his verdict: the final evidence was sufficient to dispel the idea that there had been a stampede. Also, absolutely nothing suggested that a certain section of the populace had been targeted. For better or worse, the coroner said, the names of the victims represented a thorough sampling of the people of the East End.

Nevertheless, a number of Fascist slogans appeared overnight on walls and doorways. There were a few injuries and arrests and the mood of a demonstration without the chaos of one. McNeely hoped the service would dispel the tension.

The afternoon arrived overcast and foggy. The ceremony was to begin at four o'clock, and by three-thirty the nave was full. People began to fill the aisles, sides first, then the centre. McNeely greeted officers of the local council, two local MPs, and sizable contingents of the St. John Ambulance Brigade, the Red Cross Nursing Association, the local police. Groups sitting together in pews that looked full were asked to squeeze together to fit in two or three more people. At five minutes to four, the vestibule began to fill with the overflow of people, and McNeely worried late arrivals wouldn't even be able to get in the door, precipitating horrible memories of that night, which he was trying to mend. Still, no one seemed upset or anxious. The crowd easily numbered a thousand, but grief had made them slow and solemn. At ten past four, McNeely squeezed through the back of the crowd and looked outside. No one was waiting. He offered a short prayer of thanks and closed the door.

The bishop of the diocese spoke first, and the point of his rather simple sermon was to establish a connection between the damaged church they were in—he gestured at the plain glass windows, the splintered organ—and the damaged people in the pews. McNeely watched heads pop up here and there as his congregation looked around at the mended rafters, the taped windows. He hoped the bishop wouldn't take the idea too far; no one wants to look at the physical evidence of war or imagine it applied to them. Some in the parish might remember when the church had looked worse: walls sheared off, part of the roof gone. McNeely had made repairs himself as much as he could and applied for public money for the rest. But the eye wants to complete a picture, not tear it down. At bomb sites he'd heard people talk about the books that should have been on shelves, or where a certain table had been, while standing before the open shell of a house. The bishop was reminding them of what had been lost.

A reading from Corinthians followed, then a psalm, and at that point McNeely noticed the congregation beginning to shift in the pews. A few people started whispering. A series of family members of people killed in the accident spoke next, including a woman who'd lost her husband and daughter, a man who'd lost his wife and two sons; and maybe it was because of the bishop's sermon, but when these poor people stood at the pulpit, all you could see was the damage, what had been lost. This man had had two young sons. The father spoke so softly, the murmuring in the church grew louder. The temperature inside was rising, shoes began to scrape the floor, and then a man near the back—it's always near the back; if you're going to say something incendiary, you want to know what's behind you—stood up and cried, "Your sons deserve a public inquiry!"

The interruption startled the grieving father.

"Some of the dead were the only remaining relatives of soldiers overseas!" someone else yelled, an unbearable detail recently reported in the press. Heads swung back to the pulpit, where the poor father still stood. He looked concerned, unable or unwilling to be the leader the crowd now craved. The congregation grew still, waiting to see what was going to happen.

"But Morrison won't tell the soldiers!"

The suggestion that the government would try to hide the accident from these soldiers at the front proved too much. The idea coursed through the room, a visible wave, a contagion. It brought a number of people to their feet. Those in the aisles pressed forward. McNeely signalled desperately to the violin soloist, next on the programme, but she shook her head furiously.

"It's the mayor's fault!"

McNeely scanned the crowd but didn't see the mayor.

"Gowers is an ass!"

Shouts and yells began to echo through the church. More than half the people were standing now and in an instant crossed a threshold, abandoned some notional boundary of how one should behave in church. McNeely could feel it. A moment ago decorum reigned, even as the crowd grew passionate. Now a cacophony of insults and accusations filled the nave. Some people near the front were fighting, and on the right a group was trying to press towards one of the exits.

McNeely ran to the pulpit. The father made way for him, and

McNeely cried out, "See us!" in a voice so loud and strong, it surprised him.

The crowd quieted a notch, and he took a breath and did it again.

"See us!"

Some of the faces turned towards him showed confusion and anger. But these were not the majority. Most were open, scared, curious about the voice directing them. He felt a jolt run through him.

"That is what you want! To be seen!"

More calm, more quiet. A few people in front sat down.

"To be seen enduring and behaving well, even though your homes are a shambles and your shelters are not safe."

They were listening. He had a bit of a sermon prepared on the idea that crowds, while sometimes unruly, can also be moved to heroic extremes, but he saw that it would be too wordy, too rational. He had to appeal directly to their emotions.

"You have been victims, but you've been made to feel like villains!" There was still some movement in the crowd, but they turned towards him now and strained to hear. He lowered his voice.

"You are victims, not villains! And you can be heroes by standing together and waiting. Wait for the inquiry to finish. Let justice be done." There was a lone, timid cheer, followed a second later by another one. "It won't be long. Give the report time. You won't be forgotten, or asked to endure more without help."

Most were sitting again, even the people in the aisles.

"And your dead will be remembered. That's why we are here."

He nodded at the soloist, who, after a moment, pulled her cardigan close, took a gulp of air, and made her way to the front to play. As the beautiful notes filled the church, McNeely was shaking from his knees to his shoulders, but the storm had passed. He could hear the sounds of people settling down, straightening their coats, quieting children. He allowed himself to breathe in relief and caught the eye of Constable Henderson, sitting near the back. The man looked quickly away, thinking perhaps, as McNeely was, of the powerful sedative effect of just one authoritative voice in a moment of turmoil.

By the time the pavane ended, McNeely was able to walk steadily to the doors of the church. He led the congregation out of St. John's and past the shelter entrance. The crowd bulged there, as people paused to look, but it did not stop. McNeely saw Ada Barber with the new baby and took her hand. She started to say something about what had happened inside the church, but he couldn't hear her. Surrounded by friends and neighbours, families complete and incomplete, they followed the Roman Road to Globe Road and turned left. They took Sugar Loaf Walk through the field and crossed Victoria Park Square. McNeely had intended to bring them out to Cambridge Heath and then turn left back to the church, but the children, giddy from the service and the dancing candles, ran into the Museum Gardens. Within a few moments, the event lost its sense of direction but not its purpose. Many people were smiling.

Ada had begged Tilly to come with her and the baby. The candle-lit march, even in daylight, was something she would have loved, but she refused. She chose to sit on their windowsill and watch the day fade from there. She could just see the tip of St. John's steeple.

She spent most of her time on thresholds now. Doorways, landings, windowsills. From her current perch she could see up and down Jersey Street. The house directly across from them was gone. On their side of the street, the houses three, five, and ten doors down were heaps of dust and broken masonry, piles of rubble not yet cleared that spilled into the street like piers along a beach. Damaged houses showed new pink tile repairs as bright and obvious as scar tissue. The foggy afternoon gave way to a clear evening, a weather reversal Tilly found oddly discomfiting. She did not like the late-day clearing, and it was not just because of the planes. It had to do with getting used to something, only to have it change.

She put herself to bed, and when Tilly woke in the morning, there was a small white stub of candle next to her pillow.

Thirty-two

Laurie recalled Clare Newbury. She had medical training and had helped with the casualties in the booking hall the whole of the night in question, so he thought he would talk to her again.

"Everything all right?" he asked as she arranged herself in the chair.

"Yes, sir."

"Nothing changed since the last time we talked?"

She hesitated but then shook her head. "No, sir."

"I'd like to make sense of one thing, if I could. How did some people survive at the bottom of the crush while others did not? I think it's the reason the accident is so troubling."

"Among many, I'd say." She spoke sharply.

"Indeed."

"I'm sorry. It has been a bit of a strain to get everything back to normal."

"I understand. No apology necessary. For example, these babies that people handed out of the stairway. In your opinion, could it have been a mother's strength that kept them safe? Something about the architecture of her body?"

"Not all mothers saved their children that night, Mr. Dunne."

"Yes, but . . ."

"So why propagate such a story?"

"Are you a mother?" he asked.

"I have certainly seen how this tragedy has affected people."

He almost asked her how it was possible, then, to not search for a story. The crush had not filled the landing. The people had been crushed only against themselves.

"Perhaps I can't explain it," he said, defeated. "Let me ask you something else. You have a lot of experience in this shelter. Do you have anything to say about the stairs?"

"They were very dark."

"I understand there was a light."

"Yes, but it was dim, when it was there."

"When it was there?"

"It got smashed sometimes, and, you know, I think some of the wardens were tired of replacing it."

"I see. All right. Thank you very much for coming back."

"Sir, before I go. I think you've spoken to Bertram Lodge, one of the town hall clerks?"

"I remember him."

"He's having a great deal of trouble."

"Is he?"

"He feels awful about being in the crowd that night."

"I seem to remember he had some difficult work to do after the accident, as well."

"Yes. Is there anything else he could do? Is there some way you could use him?"

"I'll give it some thought."

"Did you have difficulty breathing where you were?" Laurie asked.

"No."

"Try and think back. When the rocket gun or whatever it was went off—"

"Yes."

"—were you pushed forward?"

"I was pushed into a mass of people; it was something solid."

"In other words, it seems to you that the block in front that caused the people to stop had occurred before the rocket gun went off?"

"It's hard to say, sir."

Thirty-three

After the memorial service, which cheered her, Sarah Low invited Clare and Bertram to come round for tea. She planned a cold-weather menu, pork chops and potatoes. She also tried scones with potato flour, but they came out of the oven heavy and small. Nevertheless, she put them on a rack to cool and hoped they might taste sweeter than they looked. She didn't mind. She had lots of energy, now that James had agreed to her plan.

She plumped the sofa and folded up the rug so that the chairs would sit evenly around the table. She lifted the drop leaves and secured them with two pieces of wood James had cut for the purpose. She took out her lace cloth. Bertram and Clare would sit at the ends, she decided; she and James would sit side by side, facing the wall. That was best. It would give their guests a view of the room.

Sarah was setting out the candles when James came in from the garden. He looked tired. "Isn't it a little early for vegetables?" she asked.

"Yes."

She'd hoped for a denial. She thought he might tell her something about gardening she didn't know, and it worried her that this was not the case.

"I think a late frost is the least of our problems," he said.

She shook her head. She would not acknowledge that everything was as bad as he said. "Go and get changed."

He turned to go but then stopped. "It looks nice, Sarah. You're a fine hostess."

She smiled and waved him into the bedroom.

Clare and Bertram arrived on time with a small bouquet. Clare was wearing a fashionable green dress tied at the waist. She'd heard Sarah's news at the canteen and gave her a meaningful hug. James breathed, "Bertram," and clapped the sad and pale boy to him. As they turned into the room, Sarah tried to make a joke about the trouble they must have been put to in carrying the flowers any distance, Morrison likely to expand his ban any day to all forms of flower transport, even walking.

They all smiled, but not as widely as they might have. Nothing seemed out of the realm of possibility.

The pork chops were good, the potatoes bland. Bertram and Clare refused seconds. Sarah told them not to worry—this was a special occasion, the Potato Plan be damned—but they declined again. Conversation veered from food to flowers to the recent rally at Trafalgar Square for a new European front. They'd all gone to see the Lancaster bomber there, which was drawing the biggest crowds since the coronation.

After the meal, Sarah cleared the table and put on the kettle. Clare stacked the scones on a plate. There was nowhere to withdraw to, so when everyone was once again seated around the table, chairs pulled up, laps and napkins smoothed, Clare cleared her throat and said, "James? Have you and Bertram had a chance to talk about the shelter?"

Both men shook their heads. Then Bertram said, "I had to do an inventory." Outside, a woman called and another woman answered. Sarah poured more tea.

"Of all the items in the victims' pockets," Clare explained. "Do you think they were looking for something?"

James shook his head. He didn't know.

"Have you been back to the shelter?" Bertram asked him.

"No," he said slowly, not adding that he was pretty sure he'd never walk to the shelter again. Tragedy pockmarked the neighbourhood as badly as the bombs: the corner where he'd seen a woman step in front of a car driven without headlights in the blackout; the garden where a man was impaled on a fence by a bomb; the pile of rubble where he and Sarah had heard the baby crying. And now the shelter. But every person in war had an archive like this. You just left people alone with it. There was nothing else to do.

Bertram said he had not been back, either. "What happened?" he asked, and the room went still.

"I changed the lightbulb, if that's what you mean," James said.

"You did?"

"Yes, God damn it!"

"James!" Sarah said. She turned to Bertram. "I'm sorry."

The two women's voices outside settled beneath the front window, and their conversation, about kitchen paint, suddenly filled the room. When they'd moved on, Sarah said, "I don't think Bertram means anything, James. He's as confused as the rest of us."

"I wasn't very close to the entrance," Bertram said. "I mean, I was back in the crowd. I don't know how far back. I think about it a lot, actually, where I was." He looked down.

James stared. "Why? Did you push? Just like the rest of them?"

"James! Stop it!" Sarah stood up, her face pale. She flapped her hands in front of her. "Clare, will you help me clear? I'm sorry."

"Of course."

When the women were in the kitchen, Bertram spoke quietly. "I tried not to."

James looked horrified. "I'm sorry, Bert. I don't know what's wrong with me."

Sarah and Clare came back into the room, Sarah's face stern. "You are both asking yourselves questions that needn't be asked," she said. She looked at James, then turned to Bertram. "There are horrors enough in this war without imagining more. You were in a crowd of hundreds."

Bertram nodded, then stood. "Let me show you," he said.

Clare put her head in her hands. "His list," she said. "I don't know what to do."

Bertram brought back the frayed and dirty notebook. He turned the pages, and at first everyone read silently; then Sarah pointed to a name she recognized and laughed at the thought of one particular woman with a packet of seeds in her pocket. "But she hated gardening!"

James smiled. "That's right. I'd forgotten."

The mood in the room eased a bit, and Sarah, enormously relieved, went to the kitchen to pour out some brandy.

When Clare and Bertram had gone, Sarah settled James on the couch. She made him a cup of tea, but when he didn't sip it, she said, "Would you like to go to the pub? You haven't been in a while."

He looked at her as if from a distance, then shook his head.

She picked up her mending. "Don't think about it anymore. It'll be all right. Clare and Bertram know you."

He nodded.

Her hands dropped to her lap. "What about our plan?" She tried not to sound too eager. "Shall we go to the orphanage tomorrow?"

It meant everything to her when he smiled. "Yes. That will help, won't it?"

She could not help grinning. "Oh, I think so. A baby is just what we need. You'll see."

Thirty-four

In the corner shop Paul couldn't find the orange juice. It was some time before he realized this was because he was standing in the freezer section. He moved down the aisle to the relatively colder area of open refrigeration, and there they were, the juices. So pleased was he with the progress of his day, his interview with Dunne, that he bought two bottles, in spite of the astonishing price. It seemed Mrs. Loudon was right. Nearly fifty pence. He also bought a packet of tea and a bar of Cadbury's chocolate and asked the clerk at the counter to put all of it in a nice bag. He felt kind, magnanimous, happy to celebrate the fact that he seemed to be drawing Dunne out.

"What? We haven't got those."

"Bags?"

"Not good ones."

"What about ribbon?" Paul asked.

The clerk showed him a ball of twine.

When he got back to the B and B, Paul used the piece of twine the clerk had grumpily handed over to tie a bow around the bag. He wrote *Thank You* on the side and left the whole package on the counter for Mrs. Loudon, who was out. He took his other groceries, some beers and a bag of crisps, and went upstairs to his room.

The first thing to do was call Tilly. He didn't want the Bethnal Green project to go much further without talking to her, but they were not particularly close. She hadn't been very interested in him when they were growing up, though he'd always had the sense that she was looking out for him, protecting him, from—among other things—their unhappy parents.

She answered, whispering.

"The boys asleep?" Paul asked.

"Just. Owen's got an ear infection."

This was the way Tilly had once explained to Paul what had happened during the war: by sharing something that was in short supply, the truth, she'd gained something else in short supply, a sibling. It didn't make any sense in peacetime, she'd said when he asked her to be more specific, but she was very glad to have a brother. She'd been married, briefly, to a city engineer and had two sons: five-year-old Owen and two-year-old Michael.

She was quiet when Paul told her about the film. "Tilly?" he said. "You there?"

"How long have you been working on this?"

"I don't know, a few years."

"Have you talked to Laurie Dunne?"

"In fact, I'm calling from Stockbridge. He's agreed to participate." Paul waited for a response. "Hello, hello?"

"I'm here."

"Is something wrong?"

"I wish you could do a film about something else."

"I'm pretty committed, Tilly. What do you remember about Dunne? He interviewed you, right?"

"Oh, it was such a long time ago."

"But you must remember something."

"The room was hot and smelly. There were cobwebs on the windowsill. I think I sat up there; I have no idea why now."

"Was Mum there?"

"What do you mean?"

"Was Mum there when he interviewed you? It would have been pretty scary for an eight-year-old alone."

"I'm always surprised by what other people assume is scary. No. I was on my own."

Paul nodded. That was the Tilly he knew, almost always on her own. He pictured her in Islington, quietly organized, dressed simply, probably in jeans. She wore her hair, against the fashion of the day, cut short, and her skin, ruined by poor nutrition during the war years, was always rough and red on her cheeks.

When he told her that Dunne had given him a new piece of information, she said sharply, "What is it?"

Warden Low's suicide made her gasp.

"Dunne covered it up," he said. "It was reported as a stroke."

"I'm sorry. I have to go."

"Wait. Why?"

She said suddenly, "You want to know our big secret, then? I'm the child who spoke to the newspaper reporter. I told him a woman fell. I broke the story."

"I didn't know that." He could hear her sniffing and wiping at tears.

"The money was nice. Mum used it to pay the orphanage for you."

"You were bribed?" Paul asked.

"I don't remember how much. I have to go."

"Wait. You saw the first woman? Did you know she was a refugee?"

"No."

"That's what Dunne told me today. He covered that up, too."

"Has he told you anything else?"

"Not yet," Paul said.

Tilly was crying. "Are you going to talk to him again?"

"Tomorrow."

"Then I have a message for him." He could hear her trying to catch her breath. "Tell him I say hello. Tell him I wish him well. Will you do that? Will you see if he remembers me? Tell him I have never discussed it and I don't think he should, either." Despite her efforts, she was sobbing.

Paul sat on the edge of his bed, completely still. He'd rarely heard her cry. "Of course. All right. Tilly, please don't cry. I'm sorry. What have you never discussed?"

Thirty-five

By the time Ross brought Tilly, the room was fast losing light. Outside, the sound of starlings echoed in the street like glass breaking and falling, a flock filling the trees along the lane.

"Mrs. Barber," Ross said. "You have to come with me now."

"Why?" Ada grabbed Tilly's hand and raised her chin at Laurie. "He said I could stay."

The girl spoke before Laurie could. "It's all right, Mum."

Ada searched the girl's face, evidently relieved to hear her voice. "Really? It is?" She held her at arm's length, then hugged her. When she held her at arm's length again and the girl nodded, Ada wiped her tears and went out.

Laurie smiled at Tilly. She had a sweet chin-length bob and dark brown eyes. "Well," he started. "Your name is Tilly Barber?"

She nodded.

"And you live at Three Jersey Street with your mother and father? I think it's your mother I've just been speaking to."

"That's right. Can I sit on the windowsill?"

Laurie agreed, and after the girl had jumped up there, he turned his chair slightly towards her.

"Right." He abandoned his plans to begin with a question about school or her favourite films. Still, she was a child, and something in him needed to explain. "This is an inquiry, as you know, into the events of the Tube-shelter disaster on the third of March. Your mother has told us that she was on the stairs that night with you. Could you tell me in your words what happened?"

Tilly blew on a small cobweb, first gently, then harder, sending the spider hopping.

"You and your mother were two of the last ones out of the stairwell," Laurie said. "You must have been very brave."

Tilly looked up and frowned. "Did you know Mrs. W.?" she asked.

"Mrs. Wigdorowicz?"

The girl nodded, and Laurie took a chance. "A little."

"She was nice."

"Yes."

Tilly nodded and seemed to decide something. "She was in front of us."

"All right."

Then Tilly raised her hands to indicate just where Mrs. W. had stood. Directly in front of them. So close they could touch her. After a moment Tilly straightened her arms hard in a pantomime of what happened next. The movement was forceful and abrupt and pulled her off the windowsill. Confused and embarrassed, her eyes burning from not blinking, she waited and stared straight ahead.

"Others have said it was too dark to see anything," Laurie said.

Tilly didn't move.

"Are you sure?"

She nodded. "We could see. The stairs are dark, but there are always one or two people with torches."

Tilly turned back to the web, this time blowing so hard, it came unmoored. The spider scurried up the window to the ceiling.

Laurie rubbed his face. Was it possible? Was this what had turned the crowd that night? He'd hoped to find something, but it never occurred to him it would be this. One woman pushing another, a Jew, on the stairs.

"What happened next? What happened to Mrs. W.?"

She shook her head. Laurie wasn't sure if she didn't know or didn't want to speak anymore.

"Tell me, Tilly, until just that moment, had you heard any loud noises or bangs? Anything unusual that you hadn't heard before?"

She shook her head. "That came after. I think. I'm not sure about that."

"All right. Thank you. We'll look into this further."

The child nodded gravely, and after she'd gone, Laurie shared with Ross his opinion about the reliability of children as witnesses. Ross agreed.

The final witness shook but didn't cry.

"I heard a man say, 'I can't breathe.' I don't know where he was. I couldn't talk by then. I could hear other voices, but they seemed far away. I had my little boy with me. I was holding his hand, and he was next to me on the stairs—he was only three—but when we started falling, I must have pulled him in front of me. I don't know how. He was beneath me. I tried to give him room. I thought if he would just turn his head . . .

"After the all-clear sounded, we still couldn't move for a long time. Then we were out of it. They were laying out the bodies in the station, and I found him there. He'd lost a shoe."

Thirty-six

It was easier to abandon his reticence on the subject of Bethnal Green than he'd imagined. Indeed, Laurie noted with curiosity how much he wanted to discuss Ada and Tilly; the poor, lost clerk Bertram; Warden Low, too, though he couldn't bear it for long. He could still picture the inquiry room, large and pleasant, but worried that when he saw it again in the film, he wouldn't recognize it. It might be a community centre by now, or a nursery school.

Laurie and the mighty William had come for what was now billed as an "old-fashioned" lunch. Both men suspected these events were numbered, for a variety of reasons. He took a sip of claret and nodded at Smith, who limped into the grill room, his knee still bandaged from the tent disaster. Smith would have taken the nod as a sign of Laurie's sympathy, but it pleased Laurie to see evidence that Smith was still required by more than the rules of the club to stay out of the river. When he turned back to William, he heard that the seven-year-old granddaughter, Lucy, big sister of new baby Will, was getting a pony for her birthday.

Laurie sighed. It was not that he didn't want to hear about his friend's grandchildren; it was that every time they came up, Laurie searched William's eyes for some sign that he understood the sad predicament of Laurie's life. No children, no promise of grandchildren. He had one good report to his name, a handful of legal decisions. He had helped rebuild Coventry Cathedral after the war. These were his legacies. In Coventry, he and Armorel had worked alongside a number of young Germans. They didn't say much to each other, but they didn't have to. The fingerprints on the stones were enough. Maybe he'd visit the church again. Maybe Barber would want to film there.

He and William ate in silence for a few moments, until William said, "You'd rather I didn't talk about the children?"

Laurie stared. He heard the next words in his head before he said them and was surprised. Had the times affected him more than he'd thought?

"I just wonder, William, if you ever consider my feelings on the matter?"

William swallowed. He apparently did not have the new vocabulary at his disposal, and Laurie dearly wished he had let the whole thing be.

"Never mind," he said quickly. "What kind of pony is Lucy getting?"

William smiled, and just like that, the subject was history, as if nothing had ever been said. This, at least, men of their age could still manage. The sea of disappointment inside Laurie began to subside, the cold depths settling, smooth and glassy once again.

When he next had a chance, during the main course, he told William about Barber, the interviews, the retrospective he was planning. He wanted to ask William what he thought of such exercises, though he thought he knew what his friend would say:

The risk is the story being sensationalized for a modern audience.

(Of course.)

The reward will be proof that your work is still relevant.

(Yes. Quite nice. Let's have a drink to celebrate.)

But before he could speak, William coughed and said, "A retrospective? Wasn't that all done with a long time ago?"

Laurie stared. "Done with?"

"Well, I mean, wasn't that your claim to fame, as they say?

A bit dismal to relive our glory days. Wasn't there a programme before?"

"No. This is the first."

William must have heard the annoyance in his voice. He wiped his mouth and sat straighter. "Good, then," he offered. "Don't suppose they could manage it without you. The report was groundbreaking for its time, wasn't it?"

Laurie ordered the cheesecake for dessert and moved off into the den for coffee.

William found him some time later, dozing over a newspaper. He sat down and surprised Laurie with a question. "Look, Lucy's parents want to know if you'll be Will's godfather."

"But they don't know me."

"They know about you."

Laurie said his reputation as a magistrate hardly qualified him for such ecclesiastical duty.

"Because you're my friend," William said, and then Laurie was embarrassed because it seemed the request was coming from him and he meant it.

"This one is to be mine," William explained. "In a sense. Named for me. I asked."

"I see." Laurie drank some coffee and considered. "Well, then, no."

William was shocked.

"I no longer offer moral guidance, you see. All done with a long time ago."

William stared. "You needn't be like that."

Thank goodness for the documentary, Laurie thought. It felt like something new in his pocket, just when everything else in his life had turned old and dull.

After William had gone, Laurie glanced around the den. He hoped Barber would need half a dozen interviews or more, William be damned. And with the boy tomorrow, he would speak more definitely. Hadn't he earned the right to speak in pro-nouncements? It was an absolute surprise to him that the report had become his lasting achievement. He'd known it was impor-tant at the time, but that it would be the main work in a life lived over so many decades? He wished someone had warned him. He'd tried to bring to later problems the same mixture of empathy and insight he was supposed to have had in Bethnal Green, but it seemed he never again had the two in quite the same proportion. Sometimes he'd had insight but his empathy was off. Other times empathy flooded him but his reasoning grew confused. Like a mathematician in decline, he could only remember how it had felt to work at his best; the ability was gone.

As he watched the waiters come and go with drinks and mints, he began to doze off in the chair. Maybe he'd find a copy of the report and reread it. He could edit it and annotate the margins, change what he wanted. Right or wrong, that should be a bene-fit of old age.

Thirty-seven

Laurie and Ross met at the town hall for a final review of the shelter. On the way there they talked of their families. Ross told Laurie his wife had evacuated to Hertfordshire with their young children. Laurie said his daughter was home, in bed with pneumonia. He was about to mention his son when he realized he was too anxious about Andrew to do so.

"You have a boy, too?" Ross asked after a moment.

Laurie nodded.

Wet cobblestones reflected white in the sun, and here and there forsythia was beginning to bloom, yellow bursts in front of broken buildings. Laurie watched the passersby, their cheeks red and chapped, eyes watery and bright. They tied their scarves in bunches around their necks, but their bodies and overcoats were thin, leaving them strangely top-heavy. Queues everywhere were long. He thought of how in testimony, many of the people said the crowd the night of 3 March had shared a quiet sense of purpose. Of course others—the authorities, mainly—insisted the crowd was unruly, out of control. The discrepancy between these accounts bothered him.

In front of the shelter, Ross spoke with the constable on duty, while Laurie looked at the new handrails and bulkhead light, now ensconced in a steel cage. If only someone had treated the local council's plan for a new entrance as more than a routine application for the expenditure of public funds. But was everyone supposed to live with a mind full of potential horrors? He walked slowly down the steps, painted now with whitewashed strips along both sides and the centre, until he stood at the bottom of the first flight, looking back up towards the entrance. The sunlight made a jagged geometric pattern along the left side, and in the sky above the entrance, he could just see the white, shuttered cupola of St. John's. The stairs were relatively new but looked old. They seemed to him apologetic, but perhaps that was just the effect of the new paint and his imagination. The cement was damp, as if recently cleaned, and the metal handrails had a seawater smell that transferred to his hand as he walked back up. A torn sandbag hunched nearby, half its contents strewn about in anticipation of more snow.

As Ross and Laurie walked back in front of St. John's, they saw the vicar sweeping the church steps.

"Reverend McNeely," Ross said. "He's been quite a lot of help since the disaster."

When they approached, McNeely looked up and smiled. "Mr. Dunne," he said. "I'd been hoping to see you around the area a bit more. I've wanted to meet you."

Laurie liked the man's eyes, dark and full of what struck him as an unusual mixture of wisdom and worry.

"We're very eager for your report."

Laurie nodded.

"We're desperate for a story, you see."

"I've thought of that," Laurie said, just as Ross said, "Reverend, with all due respect, we're not telling stories. The report will be the truth."

McNeely smiled at Laurie. "I do hope then that the truth won't be the one I heard in the pub yesterday. A new German weapon is to blame, they say. A beam that incinerates everything for miles around."

"How can they think that?"

"Nothing burned," Ross said incredulously.

"We listen better than we observe, obviously," said McNeely. "It's the only explanation for the persistence of rumour."

"Were you near the crush?" Laurie asked.

McNeely shook his head. "God spared me a role."

"You have certainly played a role," Laurie said.

"I don't know." McNeely squinted at his church in the sunlight. The doors needed paint; the broken weather vane dangled. "I don't know what it means." He turned back to Laurie. "Maybe you'll come for a service some time?"

"I'd like to. Perhaps after the report is published, if the area will still have me."

McNeely smiled. "Forgiveness without understanding is like faith without proof," he said. "Difficult, but many in Bethnal Green are quite good at it, I've found."

Ross and Laurie continued west on the Bethnal Green Road. They passed a greengrocer's with some bunches of bananas on display, and Ross, recognizing an opportunity, pointed at them. "These are rare around here. I'd like to buy a few, if you don't mind." Laurie agreed, and they stepped inside. Tilly Barber stood behind the counter.

"Is your mother here?" he asked.

The girl shook her head.

Ross paid for his bananas, and Laurie glanced around the shop. "Well, what else is good?"

"The potatoes are freshest," she said. "Nothing else, really."

"Half a pound, then." He studied her face. "Do you remember before the war?"

"A little bit. My sister—" Tilly stopped and put her hand over her mouth. It was her mother's gesture.

"Go ahead."

"My sister didn't. She never saw the moon."

"Because of the blackout."

Tilly nodded.

"Did you describe it to her?"

Tilly nodded again.

"Often?"

"Yes."

"Oh, then you were a good big sister. She was lucky to have you."

Tilly smiled.

Thirty-eight

Although he'd promised to arrive earlier, Bertram came home from the Salmon & Ball near midnight, drunk. He was carrying, and stroking extravagantly, a small, underweight cat. Wary of his welcome, he stayed by the door, his coat on.

"They say it's blind," he said softly. "The blokes down the pub."

Clare came over and touched the warm, slightly damp ears. It was raining outside, and the animal, Bertram explained, had insisted on keeping its head out of his coat on the way home. Clare lifted the cat out of his hands and put it on the floor.

"It's been hanging around the pub since the accident," Bertram said.

Clare watched the animal exploring the room, moving in a decidedly less fluid way than most cats she'd seen. It was a tortoiseshell, the fur a motley pattern of orange and black and white. The face, particularly, seemed mismatched, half-orange, half-black, with some white around one side of the mouth, almost as if it were wearing a mask that had been bumped askew.

"That doesn't make any sense, Bert. They linked it to the accident so that you'd take it. Why would the accident have blinded a cat?"

Bertram shrugged and weaved. "I just thought I'd bring it home. That way if something happened to me, you'd have it to take care of."

Clare looked at the animal again. "I don't like cats."

"Oh."

Clare hung up his coat and walked him to the sofa. Bertram's dreams—heavily populated and full of voices, he'd told her—were leaving him tired and sad. She knew the regulars at the Salmon & Ball had started saving a stool for him at the end of the bar. She'd seen it. The stool had two full-length legs at the back and two shorter ones at the front to accommodate the step up to the back room. The game was to get the bloke who sat there to drink too much, forget, and push himself back from the bar, with predictable results. Bertram hadn't disappointed them yet.

"Bertram," she said. "You've got to stop this."

"Why don't you like cats?" he asked, bleary, innocent.

She stroked his cheek. "They're too independent." Bertram nuzzled his head into her hand. He was falling asleep.

She smiled and ruffled his hair, waking him. His eyes opened, and she told him Mr. Dunne had requested his list. She saw the news slowly permeating the drink. He smiled.

"This is what you've been waiting for, Bert," she said.

"I'll take it tomorrow."

She had things she wanted to tell him. She thought of waking him up with coffee. She could turn off the lights and open the window; a blast of cold air might bring him back. But while she was thinking, he tipped to the right, fast asleep. She settled his head on a pillow, took off his shoes. She covered him with a blanket, then turned off all the lights, opened the heavy curtain, and sat on the sofa by his chest.

She loved this reversal of the blackout—black inside and out, so that you could open your curtain. It felt like bending the rules, although it wasn't, as long as you didn't forget and turn on a light. The blackout seemed to her useless; surely the German pilots knew how to find London and her landmarks by now. Yet every night the city turned itself into a dark blanket beneath the sky, hiding and waiting.

How do you black out a home? She'd thought a lot about it at the start of the war. How do you blot out every bit of light and warmth? Bertram said you had to think of yourself as an animal or an insect, a drone of some kind, working away at the edges of a honeycomb. Fill this crack, gnaw, gnaw, cover that gap. In those days of the war, everything was preparation; spirit and determination ran high. But the blackout materials were heavy and inconvenient, and once the blackout became a reality, many just kept their windows darkened all the time. Now sometimes even she didn't open the curtains during the day.

She leaned over and kissed Bertram's lips. They tasted sweet, a little beery. She thought of his notebook, his careful record, the way he'd cared for the last carried objects of a group of people in a particular time and place. "It's war work, Bert." She pressed her hand to his chest, hoping he would feel the warmth in his sleep. "Just as much as anything else. You did it."

She put a bowl of milk out for the cat, lay next to Bertram, and went to sleep. In the morning, Bertram was gone, and the cat was licking her hand, hungry again. He'd left her the notebook for Dunne and a pair of shoes with beautiful green soles that looked almost new.

Thirty-nine

By the end of the inquiry, Laurie had called and examined eighty witnesses and imagined the night of 3 March so many times that when he closed his eyes, he heard the pounding of feet slowing from a run to a walk to a shuffle. He saw girls with long plaits, boys in short trousers, the hands of mothers trying to keep them moving.

The weather remained cold and grey, most often the sky nothing but layers of cloud. Laurie's notes were scattered wildly; his hair and clothes were a mess. When Armorel brought the tea tray, he would pat his forehead, hoping to smooth the hair and his thoughts. She'd never seen him like this—he knew that. They were both accustomed to his work behaving like a good prisoner, always quiet and on schedule. It must have been his imagination, but as he worked in the study and Armorel sewed in the drawing room, it seemed the house groaned from the strain of this new battle. Or perhaps the bombs had shaken the building's foundations after all, as their friends who left had warned.

He'd interviewed shelter wardens, police constables, superintendents and inspectors, local officials and regional officials. He'd talked to ambulance drivers, light rescue workers, heavy rescue workers, and volunteers from every other service called out that night. He'd questioned medical professionals who were either on the scene or who had admitted and examined casualties at one of several local hospitals. He'd spoken to surveyors, engineers, and technical advisors. Most of all he'd tried to listen to the average Bethnal Greener, as many of them as would come before the inquiry. He let all of them talk until they were done. The airing of grievances was important—he knew the good it could do—but now his head was full, and no clear picture of the night had emerged.

On 19 March Laurie worked at home, going out only once, for a short walk in the park. He would have liked Armorel to have accompanied him, but she was busy. He'd seen many small grey boxes, ingenious creations of cardboard and felt, and assumed that meant the stitching had progressed from the countryside into Hamburg. According to the RAF, the German women were also sewing, and they were ahead. Before the war, while England was at peace, growing slow and fat on the false assurances of distance and victory, the German women had kept busy. But the landscape of Berlin had been completed, contributing to the enormously successful mission earlier in the month. Hamburg, Armorel said, was not far behind.

In the park without Armorel, Laurie counted people. He found himself compulsively counting, the numbers mesmerizing him. Ten, fifteen, twenty-five. What did those amounts look like? If he heard a bomb had killed ten people, he drew imaginary circles the next day: that woman on the bench, the man by the water, those children skipping, the boys feeding ducks. Ten people. Gone.

Even so, he couldn't make sense of one hundred and seventy-three suffocated in a heap.

At five o'clock he returned, poured himself a drink, and watched Armorel stitch. He imagined their son, Andrew, a small speck on someone else's landscape and asked if there was anything he could do to help, to speed the project along. She shook her head. The sewing, he knew, was keeping something at bay for her, the black worry that would seep in without constant work. Periodically she asked about the inquiry, and he told her what he could. Once she said, "Mothers and children should have a separate entrance at the biggest shelters, don't you think?" and he'd made a note of it.

Back in his study, Laurie put on a recording of Sviatoslav Richter playing Bach's complete preludes and fugues. He began to pair a witness's position in the crush with what he or she had considered the main cause of the disaster. If a person had been behind or in front of the mass on the stairs, he or she tended to make furious claims: a mysterious new bomb, a gas leak, a Jewish panic. If the person had been in the stairwell, there was less certainty about anything, just a terrible bewilderment. Laurie had thought the chart might bring out an essential theme, the way Richter found inner voices in Bach. He was sure there was something here about tragedy, blame, and responsibility, but he couldn't see it.

The next day it snowed. At his desk early, Laurie watched the flurries for a time, impressed by the silence. He'd never considered snow stealthy, but that was what struck him now. How could something so extensive happen so quietly? Why was the sound of rain more reassuring?

He pressed his eyes and tried to concentrate.

During the inquiry he'd filled two notebooks, thirty-five loose sheets, and one napkin from a pub on Russia Lane. All of it was a mess. Half the testimony contradicted the other. The crowd was quiet; the crowd was loud. The constables and wardens had worked hard; the constables and wardens were nowhere to be seen. There was light on the stairs; the stairs were dark. There was a loud blast no one had ever heard before; there were no unusual sounds that night. There were only a few Jews in the crowd; the crowd was filled with Jews.

He turned to the sheet in his typewriter. There he'd begun: *It will, I think, be convenient to give you at once the more important measurements of the part of the shelter involved.*

He stared out of the window again. He'd nearly recalled the

man Steadman for a second interview, to see if he could corroborate what Tilly had told them, but decided he didn't want to. He didn't want Ross to hear the story again. He didn't want to reduce the disaster to just another example of there being too many Jews in the East End. This was not the story he wanted to tell; nor was it the one the city needed to hear.

He turned back to his typewriter. *I am satisfied the wardens responded well and did what they could once the accident was under way,* he wrote. *In a matter of seconds, the jam was complete across the full width of the landing.*

Jam? Was he really going to call it a *jam?*

He thought through the sequence. The alert sounded just after a quarter past eight. Between 8:27 and 8:28 a woman fell. Would she have fallen if the stairwell hadn't been so dark? Would she have been able to get up and go on if there hadn't been so many people? The constable who should have been in place earlier didn't arrive until 8:35. By then the calamity was irreversible.

Laurie tried music, choosing his favourite recording of Beethoven's *Violin Concerto.* Melody, all melody, seemed to speak to him of the tragedy. He was listening to Chopin and Mozart, Beethoven and Brahms, their works somehow hinting at how the memory of this event would one day feel.

He turned to the newspaper clippings he'd saved, among them the story in the *Daily Herald* of 2 March about the raid on Berlin. Witnesses had mentioned many times the Halifax captain's breathless description of the mission: *A minute or two after ten o'clock, I saw the first flares drop. A cloudless sky and excellent visibility enabled the crews to recognize their exact targets on the streets in Berlin. Bomber after bomber dropped its load, and we watched the fires break out and spread until they became a great concentrated mass.*

The precision of this attack had worried the Bethnal Greeners, and by 3 March the area was preparing for a terrible German response. It seemed unfair to Laurie to label as panic such imaginative empathy. There were just too many people, all of them with these fires in their thoughts—a crowd thinks in images. Then someone fell on a dark staircase, and the rest kept coming.

He put in a fresh sheet of paper.

If the purpose of a report is to explain what caused a tragedy, then I should begin with maps and diagrams and endeavour at once to describe the particulars of the accident in detail. But if perhaps the better purpose of a report is to understand a tragedy, then I should begin with a woman in a crowd, surrounded but alone.

He sat back in his chair. These felt like the truest words he'd written so far. He stood and paced the room. He was a man who reputedly understood the lives of others, so why not start here? With this poor, overburdened woman.

She was a woman in a crowd, surrounded but alone.

It didn't sound like a report, but it was how he wanted to begin.

She was a woman in a crowd, surrounded but alone. When the crowd flowed into the stairwell . . .

He looked up to see ash and debris suddenly mixed with the snow falling over the park. Fearful for the report, this promising beginning, he stood and shouted for Armorel. He was gathering papers madly, certain that there was a fire, that they'd have to evacuate, when she ran in and assured him it was only a gardener burning the last of the winter brushwood.

She looked at him quizzically. "Are you all right?"

Relieved, he sat down. "Armorel! I'm as well as I've been in days."

He worried how he would address some of the more specious rumours and allegations. He wondered how to include some of the most useful complaints and suggestions. And yet for the first time he felt he was on the right track. He wrote a quick note to Ross, asking him to get the clerk's notebook. He would use Bertram's list. It would have details he'd need to fill out the narrative he was imagining, and it would help the boy to turn it over. He'd seen many times that people needed others to understand and accept the manner in which they tried to make amends.

Forty

When Sarah asked Rev. McNeely to visit her husband, he came immediately, expecting to find a man in bed, but Low was in the tiny back garden, working at turning the soil. McNeely's first thought was that perhaps, in her concern, Sarah had exaggerated her husband's symptoms. But when McNeely approached and saw Low's round glasses sliding down his gaunt face, he knew she had not.

Low smiled and welcomed him. It was obvious he knew why McNeely had come.

McNeely hesitated. He didn't know whether to help Low or to encourage the exhausted man to take a rest.

"I'm sure Sarah's planning tea," Low said without stopping. He squinted up at the first-floor window, where Sarah's pale face flashed and disappeared.

"She's worried about you," McNeely said.

"I know."

"Where can we sit?" McNeely asked.

Low gestured to the back step of the ground-floor flat. "They don't mind," Low said, meaning the flat's residents. "They used to sit on my bench." He pointed to the corner where an old wisteria—the last vestige of Low's former flower garden—grew. "But I used the wood for scrap some time ago."

"We'll sit on a new bench after the war," McNeely said. When Low didn't respond, McNeely lowered his voice. "James, is there anything I can do?"

"Any word from Bertram?"

"No."

"He's just gone? Where would he go?"

McNeely shook his head.

Sarah brought out the tea and left it on a small, chipped tray from which the men could serve themselves. She looked at James anxiously, but he smiled at her. She thanked McNeely for visiting, then went back inside.

"How's Clare?"

"Strong as ever." He looked at Low. "Actually, very upset. But she's keeping busy, doing a lot of drawing. I think she'll be all right." They were quiet a few minutes. Finally McNeely said, "What about you?"

"Sarah and I are planning to adopt one of the orphans."

McNeely grabbed Low's arm.

"We haven't done anything yet," Low said quickly. "There are a few things I need to get in order first."

McNeely knew he'd embarrassed Low. He took his hand away and tried to sit very quietly.

Low told him about the strange experience of sending a letter of resignation that no one appeared to notice. "At first I thought they must be busy with all the other matters related to the tragedy. But then the story got in the papers and people started to talk about the light on the stairs, and still no word from Morrison or news that I'd resigned. Then Dunne called me before the inquiry, and I thought, This is it." Low turned to McNeely, baffled.

"But nothing happened." He shook his head. "I actually began to reconsider. That night I tried going back to the shelter. It had reopened, and the deputy wardens were managing pretty well in the absence of any other instruction, but I thought I'd go back, at least until I had some kind of official word about what I was supposed to do."

"You'd like me to find out what happened to your resignation?" McNeely asked when it looked as if Low had finished.

"But do you know what happened?" Low continued. "I couldn't get there. Couldn't walk down those steps. Couldn't stop seeing all those people. I tried every day after that, and each time I turned around farther away. My own kind of creep-back, I'm afraid."

It was obvious the man was grieving, haunted. "You are not to blame for this tragedy," McNeely said.

"If I'm not to blame, then I'm not responsible for all the other nights when people were safe."

"Well, I think that's somewhat true. At some point we trust to Providence."

"You do that." Low finished his tea. "What I know is this: I replaced a lightbulb that night, pretty sure of what the people would do, but I did it anyway. I was tired of their small concerns. I knew the light could barely be seen from the street. I knew that either way it wouldn't make any difference to a German pilot!" He choked, his voice reduced to a horrified whisper. "I wanted to prove it, I think. I wanted to show them."

"This accident was not your fault," McNeely said.

Low looked up but seemed to see nothing in McNeely's face that could convince him. After a moment, he spoke again. "Please make sure the people know I sent that resignation the morning after the accident. The post seems to have let me down."

"What does Mr. Dunne say?"

"I assume he doesn't know."

McNeely smiled. He would ask Dunne some day if preparing a report for the government felt as futile as offering faith during war.

Low stood and began pulling on his garden gloves.

"James," McNeely said. "Wait for the report. It may explain more than you think."

"I'll wait," he said after a moment. "But I don't know what the report can tell me that I don't already know. I was the chief warden. The shelter was my responsibility." He looked up at his flat. He smiled and waved at Sarah. "You give something a name, and it takes on a certain size in the mind. 'Front hall', even if it's no more than two steps and a mat." He dropped his arm and looked around his modest garden. "'Arbor,'" he said, pointing at the old wisteria that arched halfway over nothing. "'Shelter.'" He stared at McNeely, his eyes wide, desperate. "How can I live with that?"

McNeely was about to answer when he saw Low look him up and down, his face suddenly changing into a sneer. "And if you are homosexual, as they say, how do you live with that?"

"You are not yourself," McNeely said.

The vicar watched Low's back and shoulders as he walked away. He could see the hurt in their angles even as Low returned to digging the soil furiously.

Forty-one

On Sunday evening Laurie told Armorel he was going to court to catch up on paperwork neglected since the inquiry. Instead he put on a coat and hat, pulled his scarf up around his face, though the evening was mild, and timed his arrival at St. John's for just after evensong, a service few would attend, he guessed. He was right. He found McNeely alone, watering the garden at the back.

"Oh, but you've missed the service," McNeely said, turning.

When Laurie didn't answer, McNeely nodded and turned back to the bed. He gestured at the spring bulbs beginning to show. "Later in the season I put vegetables in, of course, but—" He didn't know how to finish. It seemed hopeless to have to justify growing flowers. "I'm glad to see you," McNeely said.

Laurie waited while McNeely finished watering a small evergreen bed. He noticed but did not ask why he was watering it with wine.

When the cup was empty, McNeely knelt down and cleared some space around a few green shoots beginning to sprout on the site of Mary Casey Cole's ashes. Then he stood and looked up at the anxious magistrate. Dunne was taller, imperious, but they were only about ten years apart.

"Should we go in?" Dunne asked.

"Of course."

Inside they sat in McNeely's room, infused with the smell of extinguished candles and the old fireplace. McNeely poured them each a whisky, and the familiar warmth calmed Laurie. They talked about the borough and faith, music and the war. When McNeely lit the fire and refilled his glass, Laurie smiled. He was enjoying himself too much, he thought. He blamed the drink and took another sip.

"Do you think the different backgrounds of people here had anything to do with it?"

McNeely nodded, as if expecting the question. He moved forwards on his chair but didn't speak. Laurie respected the deliberation.

"No," McNeely answered.

"I heard quite a few things during the inquiry."

McNeely cringed and closed his eyes. When he opened them he spoke evenly. "Many people in Bethnal Green are from other places. All of them are interested in second chances. I think that's the main thing they have in common, but it's a lot."

"I'm considering leaving something out of the report."

McNeely stood and began pacing the small room. The space allowed a path away from the small fireplace, along the bed, around the front of the desk, and back again.

"It's not a war secret," Laurie said. "Sit down."

McNeely smiled. "Well, that's reassuring." He poured himself another drink, and one for Laurie. He sat. "All right. Tell me."

The relief of speaking was much greater than Laurie had anticipated. The words rushed out. "I think the government is hiding something about the new anti-aircraft weaponry. It's possible there was an unannounced test that night, something about which the area should have been warned. It's also possible a woman pushed one of the refugees on the stairs. This first woman to fall no one can find. I have nothing to prove the first theory, and the second comes from a hunch and the testimony of a child. If I include the rockets, I think the report will be suppressed. If I include the push, it will assign blame to no good end. The government will just use her, maybe the whole area, as a scapegoat for an accident that had nothing to do with race."

McNeely looked shocked but recovered quickly. "I thought they were opposed to scapegoats."

"Only if they hold elected office."

McNeely smiled, but Laurie looked sad. "I started out hoping to avoid blame."

"And now?"

"I don't know."

McNeely was shaking his head. "What was her motivation? The one who pushed."

"Does it matter? Do you think she intended the outcome?"

"No. Right. The people will understand that."

Laurie shook his head.

"If you don't include it, aren't you denying them a chance to forgive?"

"Do I have that power?"

"More than most, I think."

"I confess, then: I don't think she would be forgiven."

"And the government's mistake, if that's what the test was?"

"It might be disastrous at this point in the war if the people lost more faith in them."

"But how can you exclude these possibilities from your report?"

Laurie sipped his drink. "That's why I'm here."

McNeely nodded and put his head in his hands for a time. When he looked up, he had red marks on his cheeks. "It's my job to believe the woman would be forgiven. To believe otherwise would be cynical for a man in my position. And I've seen what this disaster has done to people. Some are having a hard time, but others are inspired."

"That's good to know. And it's also possible the sound many heard wasn't a new weapon but just a few boys setting off bottle rockets. With disastrously poor timing. Did you hear anything unusual that night?"

"No." McNeely poked the fire.

"For God's sake! You see? Maybe I'm just trying to leave a margin of doubt until I see or hear something irrefutable. Tilly is only eight years old."

McNeely looked up. "Tilly?"

"Do you know her?"

"I do."

"Her mother lost another daughter—"

"Yes, I know."

They sat in silence for a while, until McNeely suddenly rubbed his forehead. "You know James Low sent in his resignation?"

"Oh, yes."

"What about that?"

"It doesn't mean anything."

McNeely was quiet a few moments. He refilled his glass, stirred the fire. "What are you going to do?"

"I told you, that's why I'm here."

"So am I to give you an answer or just absolve your conscience?"

"Just? It seems like a big job to me."

McNeely smiled. "Well, it's my practice always to hope people aren't as bad as the worst thing they do." He offered Laurie another drink, but the magistrate declined. McNeely corked the bottle and put it back on the shelf.

"And perhaps we should only sometimes be held accountable for the unintended consequences of our actions," Laurie said.

"Good," McNeely said. "Sounds sensible."

Laurie considered a moment, then put down his glass. "I have to go."

McNeely nodded and moved quickly to open the door. "Still, I don't think you should omit anything. Maybe the best you can do is include everything you know. Then no one can blame you."

"But I'm not worried about that," Laurie said. He shook his head at the vicar and smiled. He knew the import of the secret he'd charged McNeely with, yet rarely had Laurie felt such confidence. "Thank you," he said. "You're a good man."

McNeely blushed and bowed.

When the magistrate had gone, McNeely washed out the glasses and straightened his room. The embers in the fireplace were still glowing when he got into bed and prayed.

"Please let me do no harm."

He had no clear idea about anything. His calling, such as it was, had seemed so much simpler before the war. Then, he'd had something to offer. A more complete vision of goodness. Now it seemed he merely legitimized the plans of others. The word "extract" came to mind. Ada had extracted his goodwill and allegiance. Would he have forgiven her if she'd told him? People think they want the whole truth, but they're far happier with only as much as they can forgive. Maybe that's why he didn't tell Laurie about Ada's plans? Did it really matter that hers was the first push that night? Every person who didn't stop trying to get into the shelter after it was clear the path was obstructed was guilty of something. Some part of the outcome was on all those hands, the fatal pressure divisible by the number of people present. An incalculable burden, the blame they all carried. That's what Bertram knew, wherever he was. What sort of document could explain that?

"May the reports of the world help us through," he prayed. That is probably what we need most, he thought. More reports. And he fell asleep thinking he was glad for the world that it had Laurie Dunne.

Two days after his meeting with the vicar, Laurie wrote his cover page.

Sir, I have the honour to report that in accordance with your written instruction forwarded to me on 10 March, I opened an inquiry on 11 March into the circumstances of the accident at a London Tube-station shelter. Eighty witnesses were examined, of whom four were re-called. The following report is the result of that inquiry.

Laurie allowed himself a glass of port and the triumph of Beethoven's *Violin Concerto*, then addressed the package to the Right Honorable Herbert S. Morrison, MP, and sent it by messenger. The date was Tuesday, 23 March, 1943.

Report

Forty-two

Paul was the second of Mrs. Loudon's guests down for breakfast. A tinny recording of Vivaldi's *Four Seasons* was playing on the radio, and a German couple in matching wool jumpers, one red, the other blue, was already seated. They had two Thermoses on the table, also red and blue, and a neat and spacious backpack at their feet. They had their hands wrapped around steaming cups of coffee, and while Paul watched, Mrs. Loudon brought out two bowls of porridge.

"Good morning!" they called.

Paul decided to serve himself from the buffet. Toast and cornflakes, some tinned grapefruit segments and tea. He had brought notes for the documentary with him and was trying to plan that day's interview with Dunne when he noticed Mrs. Loudon standing over the Germans' table, holding a paper bag tied up with twine.

"Are you sure?" she said, frowning at the contents.

The Germans shook their heads.

"Mrs. Loudon," Paul said. "That's from me." He bumped the table as he stood, nearly spilling his tea. "For you."

"Why?" she said.

"I thought I'd replace what I drank the other day. All that orange juice."

"I'm sure the High Street B and B doesn't need your charity."

If Paul had detected even a hint of what he'd expected—embarrassment or gratitude, a fleeting reappraisal—he would have let it go. But she seemed only indignant, annoyed, and he decided he'd had enough.

"You're right," he said. He took back the tea and bar of chocolate. "These aren't for you."

Laurie was pleased the kitchen was cleaner than before, and he smiled a bit when he saw that Paul had decided to wear a jacket again, though without a tie. Laurie was in jacket and tie, so the two were as close as they might ever come. A strong scent of lemon cleaner filled the room.

"I have a friend, Mrs. Beckford, who comes to clean sometimes," Laurie explained.

"That's good." Paul nodded. "You know, I saw a dead fox on the way here today. Near the road. I think of them as being so clever. They rarely get hit."

"It's true." Laurie looked around the kitchen. Lemon cleaner and dead foxes were not what he'd planned to discuss. "So, how much do you have written?"

"On the documentary? I won't fill in a lot of it until we do the interviews."

Laurie waited.

"It's about half-done."

"And you've been working how long?"

"Two years."

"Do you find writing hard?"

"What about you, Sir Laurence? You're famous for writing the Bethnal Green report in five days."

"Miserable time."

The television was on, and even with the sound turned low, the bouncing images and occasional applause of the Wimbledon final distracted Laurie. It had come down to the two players who most interested him: the American, Smith, and Ilie Nastase.

Paul sat straighter. "I'd like to go over something you said before. You mentioned that a refugee was the first to fall."

Laurie turned. "Did I?"

Paul was surprised. "You did." He waited, but Laurie remained quiet. "Well, so this is interesting for a couple of reasons. First, I wonder—"

Laurie stood and walked to an old record player in the corner of the room. He put on a record, and after some hissing and popping, a violin began. He turned up the volume so that it could be heard over the television. "Has Tilly told you about it?"

"I talked to her yesterday and she asked me to give you her regards. She said you shouldn't discuss the accident."

Laurie nodded. "And she's never discussed it with you?"

"No."

"I knew that from the beginning. Do you know this piece?"

Paul shook his head.

"Beethoven's *Violin Concerto*." Laurie listened for a minute, then abruptly lifted the needle. "The only one he wrote. I used to love it." He walked back to his chair and sat down.

"Sir Laurence, excuse me, but—"

"The refugee situation was very difficult," Laurie said. "I thought it wrong to blame a moment of fear and annoyance for the whole disaster."

"What are you talking about?"

Laurie hesitated. He glanced at the television. Nastase was angry, disputing a call. Telling Paul would take something away from the boy for ever, and yet he knew he was going to do it. Long life and disappointment gave him the right.

Forty-three

Laurie took Armorel to celebrate in the West End. Her pricked thumb was sore from the final push on the landscape, and they'd left Georgina in bed with a fever, but they were nevertheless in high spirits. He believed in his report; she believed in her landscape. As they stepped into Wheeler's, he kissed her, surprising them both.

"Great things ahead."

Armorel smiled and squeezed his hand.

But Laurie heard nothing from the government for two days. BISCUIT PRODUCTION TO BE REDUCED BY HALF, he read in the *Daily Mail*, along with the final Wings for Victory total, a staggering £162,015,869. The next time Laurie heard the home secretary's voice, it was on the radio, at a public news conference, announcing that the flower-by-rail ban would be lifted in time for Easter.

Laurie rang immediately. "When are you releasing the Bethnal Green report?"

Morrison demurred.

"I find it hard to believe that the sale of flowers is more important than the content of my report," Laurie said.

Morrison ticked and hummed. "I'm surprised to hear from you, actually."

"Why?"

"What is it? A psychological portrait? Social history? Fiction?"

"The people demanded a report, if you remember."

"I remember. They also demand flowers."

"This is absurd."

"We cannot release this."

Laurie looked out the window. "If it's a matter of some editing," he began, "perhaps I could—"

"I'm afraid not, Mr. Dunne. In addition to the fact that it dramatizes the events of a regrettable accident, the prime minister feels it favours too much the victims of just one disaster."

"The prime minister has read it?"

"I've discussed its contents with him."

"But if he read it himself, he'd understand what I tried to do."

"The prime minister feels that giving them a report, particularly this report, will advance the idea that investigations of this nature are now de rigueur."

"I see. You prefer to give them flowers."

"Exactly."

"Oh, for God's sake. Surely Bethnal Green is an exception."

"We'll say it would be incautious to release it, that it contains information vital to the running of the shelters or some such, information we can't allow to fall into enemy hands."

Furious, his mind racing with ideas, Laurie said, "What if I refuse? What if I distribute it myself?"

"Mr. Dunne! The War Cabinet has decided this report cannot be released. Imagine if the enemy read it. What a brilliant strategy for them. They've got us so scared, we're killing ourselves!"

"But the people are desperate."

"You should have thought of that and given them something they could read. This report would only disrupt the home front."

"No! It's meant to restore their hope. Without it they'll just blame you and the government." Laurie caught his breath and slowed down. "I'll publicize the rockets. I'll say that's why you won't release the report."

"I wouldn't do that." Morrison ticked and spoke slowly. "I think the better part of this conversation is over."

When Laurie did not respond, Morrison thanked him for doing an exemplary job in Bethnal Green. "That was the most important part, really. You handled them very well. You gave them the ceremony they needed, and they trusted you."

"Ceremony? This is not finished," Laurie said, and hung up.

On 26 March, Herbert S. Morrison addressed reporters in Covent Garden. "Tomorrow, daffodils from Wales!" he announced. "Flowers for Easter. The ban on flower transport by rail is no longer in effect."

When a reporter asked about the Bethnal Green report, Morrison turned serious and said he had not yet had a chance to read it.

"Mr. Dunne carried out this inquiry with thoroughness and expedition and made a lengthy and informative report. After talking with him I am satisfied that acts of culpable negligence are not properly to be included among the causes. He has also convinced me that we need not worry about the most pernicious of the rumours. It is difficult to judge how far all the factors that contributed to the accident could have been foreseen and provided against, but every precaution is being taken to ensure it won't happen again."

"When will you publish the report?" the reporter asked.

Morrison hesitated. "Many aspects of the incident concerned civil defence arrangements related to acts of war, about which it is undesirable that information should be given to the enemy. We must consider that question very carefully."

But the reporters could hear the beginning of an about-turn. "Not publishing will cause widespread misgiving in an already unhappy area. Are you prepared for repercussions?"

"If it comes to that," Morrison said, "I will put up with it for our national safety."

Picking up on Morrison's opening, another reporter said, "If we're getting flowers back, can we have weather reports again, too?"

Morrison laughed, and the reporters laughed with him. "Not so fast, mate. The war's not over."

This was certainly true. In June the English sewing circles delivered their landscape, and in July the RAF destroyed Hamburg. The firebombing was massive, the newspapers reported. German women fled the now uninhabitable city with burned parts of their children in suitcases. The pilots received commendations from the king, and wardens all over London were told to watch carefully the entrances to Tube-station shelters. A reprisal came, and the V2 flying bombs, but nothing like the crush at Bethnal Green ever happened again.

Forty-four

Just before 9:00 p.m. on Saturday, 27 March, James Low told Sarah he was going for a pint. He kissed her on the cheek (only later did she register how he'd lingered), left the house, walked to Bethnal Green Gardens, and hanged himself from a tree near a trench he'd helped dig. He was found an hour later by Constable Henderson, too late once again.

It was the time of night when the sky, in wide-open places, seems to grow both higher and more inclusive, and Henderson looked up past the body and offered a muddled hope that Low was somewhere above the broken world. The thought was faltering and strange for him. He rubbed his forehead, cut Low down, and carried him home.

In a very short time, word spread and friends came to help, including Clare, who administered a tranquillizer to Sarah and stayed through the night. The coroner, a kind man who thought Low innocent, recorded the death as a massive cerebral infarction, a significant stoppage of the flow of oxygen from the blood to the brain. He saw no need to specify what had caused the stoppage.

The death thus ruled an act of God, Rev. McNeely, who had been planning to baptize Ada's baby, found himself the next morning preparing for a funeral. He cried when he heard the news, certain of two things: that Low had died of grief and that his vicar had failed him. God promised to take away the sin of the world, but what about the suffering? What were they supposed to do with it? He shook violently while trying to iron his vestments and burned his hand.

Dozens of people followed the funeral carriage, but Bill Steadman ran ahead to gather more. He knocked on doors and windows, his heart giving him no trouble. Constable Henderson and Constable Ross were among the pallbearers. At the church, Clare Newbury sat with Low's widow. Ada Barber cradled the new baby on her lap, and Tilly, who slid down in the pew as far as she could, looked at and spoke to no one.

Low's friends had worked fast, organizing what they could: speakers, food, a few hymns. Not many could bear music, particularly singing. The human voice, its particular beauty, was too hard to reconcile with the horrors of the war. The church began to fill. People pressed themselves carefully into pews with strangers; others stood at the back and along the white walls. The flowers in the church had been placed for the baptism, lending a sweeter, more optimistic atmosphere to the affair, which began at one o'clock in the south close of St. John's.

Several of Low's former wardens spoke during the service, briefly but well. Ross described Low's impatience with those who tired of helping others. Steadman remembered him as a younger man, organizing charity drives, always collecting and distributing goods to those less fortunate. Constable Henderson wanted to speak but had drunk heavily the night before and was still taking sips from a flask in his pocket. Certain that drinking in church was a sin, he sat in the pew, miserable and dizzy, feeling more and more convinced that his own end was not far off.

Rev. McNeely lost his voice on several occasions, dabbing at his eyes each time with bandaged fingers and a scorch-marked cuff. During the eulogy he told a story about the eighteenth-century composer Joseph Haydn. The congregation knew McNeely was a lover of music, so this reference did not confuse them. His intended meaning, however, was another matter. During the first performance of Haydn's *Symphony No. 102*, McNeely said, a portion of the audience got up and moved to the edge of the stage in order to be closer to the great composer. Just then a large chandelier fell from the ceiling, landing on the empty seats. Not a single person was hurt.

"Was Haydn responsible?" he cried.

No one answered.

"If they hadn't moved, would Haydn have been blamed?"

The congregation stirred uncomfortably.

"For Christ's sake," McNeely whispered, gripping the pulpit.

People turned to their neighbours. "What?" they whispered. "What did he say?"

McNeely shook his head like a broken horse—later, the rumour was that he'd been drinking; indeed, all the pubs had been crowded for days—and stuck to the prayer book for the rest of the service. He chose readings from Lamentations and Job. It was a mild afternoon, the temperature rising, the sky clear. He looked up once after the Commendation and saw the congregation bathed in sunlight. The air, even inside the church, seemed to promise spring.

Herbert Morrison, it was said, sent flowers, though later no one could remember receiving them.

Laurie, rushing in at the end of the service, bumped into Constable Henderson, who told him the truth about Low's death before he could think better of it. Laurie, however, did not return the favour. He told everyone with whom he spoke, even McNeely, that the report was coming soon. Just a matter of administrative delays, he said, because he believed it. He had a plan. He was going to meet the prime minister himself.

And he might have done so except that upon arriving home he found Armorel sitting at the table in the dining room, a square envelope in front of her, just a bit too far away, as if pushed.

"It's addressed to you," she said.

Correct protocol for the notification of death in action: widow, eldest surviving son, eldest surviving daughter, father, mother.

Andrew had not married, did not have children. Later, Laurie would wonder what it felt like to be informed of the death of a child by a grandchild, as must have happened for so many during the war. But for him the notification came directly, and he read aloud the short, formal expression of regret from the army to Armorel in their dining room. The envelope also contained a brief report from the War Office of the details surrounding Andrew's death, a courtesy because of Laurie's position as a magistrate. German shelling had trapped the boy in southern Italy when his unit was moving positions. He'd gone back to retrieve supplies, and a building near him collapsed. No one knew his location, and he would have been abandoned but for a sentinel who heard his groans and rescued him. Andrew was on the mend when an infection set in. He died of sepsis before they could move him to more stable medical quarters. He would be awarded a posthumous medal for bravery.

As Laurie and Armorel tried to imagine these things, the unadorned facts of their son's last days, a golden afternoon turned into a clear night. At some point the alert sounded, but, as Georgina had recovered and returned to Bond Street and Andrew was dead, Laurie and Armorel had no one to keep safe. They heard planes in the distance but didn't move. Soon the all-clear came. A minor raid.

When it was long past time for bed, Armorel said, "Cassino."

"What?"

"That's what the RAF wants us to do next. They must have been heading there." She shook her head. "Elizabeth's sewing again," she said, and she and Laurie stared at each other, Laurie wondering what they might learn after the war, when more details could be released, Armorel how anyone found a way to live, let alone work, with the pain she felt in her chest.

Laurie picked up the report of his son's death and read it again.

Forty-five

"I imagine Tilly is referring to the fact that Ada Barber pushed the first woman to fall."

Paul stared. "What?"

Dunne closed his eyes. "I believe that was the start of it."

"That's not in the report," Paul said defensively.

"But I'm afraid it's true."

"Was it ever in the report? Was it in some version I haven't seen?"

"No."

"But you wrote you couldn't determine the start of it. What are you talking about?"

"I never knew Ada adopted a child afterwards," Dunne said calmly. "It's meant a great deal to me to find that out. I wish I'd known a long time ago."

Paul stared. "Why wasn't this in the report?"

"I didn't believe she was to blame."

"The report starts with a woman falling, but it never says who she is or how she fell." Paul shook his head. "Somewhere later you say very specifically that you could not determine the cause of her fall."

"Listen." It was neither a command nor a plea but something exactly in between. "The whole area would have erupted. I didn't believe Ada was a bad woman." He raised his eyebrows at Paul as if to say, Isn't that true? "The crush was not about the Jews."

Paul shook his head again. "How did you find out? How do you know this?"

"There was evidence at the time."

"What kind of evidence?"

"Testimony."

"One source?"

"More than one, I believe."

Paul stood up and walked to the windows. Growing up, he'd known Ada's flaws, but also her devotion. He tried to picture what Dunne was telling him, the busy, flustered mother he remembered, doing such a thing.

"In the report you never even mention that the woman—pushed or not—was a refugee." Paul's thoughts were gaining momentum. "Why?"

"It would have caused a great deal of trouble."

"Trouble? What do you mean?"

"I did not think it was information the city could have handled at the time."

"Or maybe you thought it wasn't important enough. Regrettable, maybe, but—"

"That's not right."

"—but not important enough to be included in the report, because she was a Jew."

"Now, stop. You are wrong about that. The people needed a report, not a judgement. I didn't want to deliver a scapegoat."

Paul thought a moment, then spoke slowly. "Would you have written the report the same way if the women's places had been reversed?"

"Of course."

"Really?" Paul straightened himself and raised his chin, both an imitation of Dunne and a gesture that managed to suggest the class and generational gulfs between them. "'Where are you from?'" he mimicked, an echo of Dunne. "'Barber. It's a common name.'" He slouched, and his usual voice returned. "And how do you know the truth wouldn't have spurred the government to do something sooner about the refugee problem?"

"There was no refugee problem! It would only have spurred them to block more from coming." Dunne stood, angry now. "It was the right thing to do at the time. Over the years I've received letters from survivors and children of survivors, and many of them express a deep gratitude for the report's approach."

"And the others?"

Dunne stared.

"Some must have dissented."

"Unanimity has never been the public's strength." Paul waited, and Laurie calmed himself with effort. "I reject the kind of answer only blame can bring. I pity those who felt—maybe still feel—the report fails because it doesn't blame anyone. They are the ones who haven't been able to put the incident behind them."

Paul spoke quietly. "With hindsight, would you change anything if you could?"

"You know what I say about hindsight?" Dunne said. "It's no kind of sight. Don't talk to me about hindsight. That's not what this is about. This is about a secret being held long enough, a good deed lost to history."

Paul's eyes went wide. "I see. Your good deed. You want to tell your side of it now, let people know what you did back in the war."

Dunne smiled. "Don't forget. I never answered your letters. You came to my door. Ever since, I've been wondering what kept Ada from telling me. Fear, I think, which is a shame. I would have been happy for her. I would have told her that I always wanted to believe people weren't as bad as the worst thing they do."

"Maybe it wasn't fear that kept her away."

Dunne tilted his head with interest.

"Maybe she simply didn't need your blessing."

Dunne squinted. "No, but she needed my protection, didn't she?"

Paul shrugged.

"The only thing your documentary audience will be thinking

about when they watch your film, Mr. Barber, is whether the report writer one day assigned to their tragedy will get the story right. Everyone wants to be an exception."

Dunne sat and leaned back in his chair. He was perspiring and looked exhausted. "Let it be said I did not run. I've fought public opinion before; I can fight it again." He drummed his fingers against his leg. "Have you ever been angling?" he asked quietly.

"No."

"I believed you," Dunne said.

"I never actually said I was an angler."

Dunne thought a moment. "Yes, I think that's right. Well, we could go tomorrow. We could meet at the club, if you like."

Paul didn't answer. He glanced at his watch.

"I have always been sorry about the warden, Low," Dunne said, his measured tone revealing that he was answering Paul's last question now. "He held himself so damn accountable. That was a tragedy I never intended."

When Paul still didn't say anything, Dunne seemed to deflate. He spoke softly. "I have studied a plan of the shelter many, many times since 1943." He shook his head. "Look, I hope it can be said we don't regret the roles history has afforded us?"

"No, though I—" Paul was about to say that he wasn't sure yet what role history had in mind for him when he remembered something. "The first woman to fall was carrying a baby."

"Yes."

"Who survived, supposedly. How old?"

"Like you," Laurie said. "Born during the war."

"But Ada couldn't have known. There were seven orphans. She didn't know which—" Paul didn't finish.

Dunne shrugged, a gesture that looked young and strange on him, but he seemed pleased with it. "I've been wondering how."

Without giving Dunne a chance to say more, Paul left.

In the hall he stopped to catch his breath. He stood before the quilt he'd passed many times, so dark and textured. Had it ever covered a bed? He couldn't imagine it. Dunne turned up the television; Paul could hear the pock-pocking of Wimbledon. He wondered who was winning: the good American or the unpredictable Romanian? He covered his eyes and pressed back tears. Had Dunne been playing him from the start? And Tilly? Did she know which baby he was?

"Doesn't matter," he said, and dried his eyes. "Either way, doesn't matter." That was what he would believe. And what was certainly true: he had his film.

Forty-six

After the funeral service for Warden Low, Ada stayed in her pew. The baby had fallen asleep in her arms, and she couldn't bear to disturb him. It was supposed to be his christening day, and she thought someone should remember that. She glanced up at the altar but couldn't bring herself to pray. She touched the soft, white linen above his wrist. It was the same dress the girls had worn.

Gradually the rest of the congregation left. St. John's popped and creaked, settling again after its latest disturbance, another wartime funeral. Somewhere Ada heard the sound of a broom. Outside, a few children were playing, and their voices echoed in the great space of the church as if from many miles and years away. When the nave was empty but for her and the baby, she noticed a bird, a magpie, resting on one of the rafters above the pulpit. Sparrows often flew in and usually made it safely back out again, but she'd never seen a magpie inside. When she looked more carefully, she saw that this one was working on a nest, a bit of paper in its beak. It hopped once, twice. They eyed each other. Then Ada glanced all around. She searched the whole church with her eyes, every shadowy corner, but couldn't find the nest or a mate.

The baby stirred, and Ada pressed her cheek to his head. Surviving some disasters, she sensed, you don't get to be happy again. You simply change, and then you decide if you can live with the change.

Retrospective

Forty-seven

The night of the retrospective, many people place phone calls to their parents or grandparents. "Do you remember this?" they ask. "This terrible accident at Bethnal Green? Why have you never mentioned it?"

"I did. I have! Don't you remember?"

"No. Tell me again."

On-screen, Bill Steadman is saying, "I remember one young man, a clerk at the town hall." He sat thinking. "An event like that"—he shook his head angrily—"it changes you. He came back to us, but he was never the same."

It is the series of interviews with Sir Laurence that mesmerizes. He is, England thinks, the diminished man of power, the bleak future of all once-bold men. He sits before the camera painfully straight, staring hard into the lens, denying he was out of touch with the tenor of his times. After the war, when the report was finally published (thanks to the relentless efforts of Clare Newbury and Sarah Low), it was briefly a success, though it revealed no great secrets. Instead the document presented a riveting narrative of the crush and showed an empathy for the terror and confusion of the night of 3 March that surprised and impressed many. The next year Dunne was knighted and made chief metropolitan magistrate, an honour and a burden on a broken man. He'd lost his son, and his daughter had died of a respiratory ailment. What the programme does not say (thanks to Paul, who felt the reassessment of Dunne was harsh enough) is that Sir

Laurence's only other significant contribution after the report was a redesign of the London police uniform in the mid-1950s. He railed publicly against the trousers, cut in a manner too flattering of the buttocks, he said. A disaster, in his opinion, at a time when the force was having so much trouble with the public toilets and baths. The emergence of homosexuality as cultural entertainment irritated and confounded him. He fixed the trousers and closed the baths at night, all in the same week.

The programme closes instead with survivor Bill Steadman. "We say it's different now, that one man alone couldn't write such a report, but I don't see our investigations today doing much better. Ada Barber may have been responsible, but she wasn't to blame. A distinction without a difference to some, but not to me."

Tilly checks on her boys again, her blood running hot with the old anguish and grief. She'd hoped never to feel this way again. She's already turned herself inside out once.

"I did not suppress the cause of the accident," Laurie had said to the interviewer. "I simply downplayed a contributing cause to save the people from relying on blame."

"Do you still believe that was right?" the interviewer probed. Tilly didn't know who he was, though Paul had said he was famous. "Didn't the people have a right to know what really happened?" The man's voice had energy and tenacity and just the slightest edge suggesting disbelief. "With hindsight, what do you say?"

Dunne cringed at the word "hindsight". "I did tell them what happened. I told them a version of the story that would give them hope. I still feel that was the right thing to do. I didn't punish anyone."

"No? What about James Low?"

Dunne didn't answer, but you could tell he thought the question unfair. Tilly did, too. She wishes she'd known more about the programme before it was broadcast, but Paul had never wanted to discuss it.

She closes the boys' door and runs to her bed, trying but failing to outrun the memory of the last time she'd seen Dunne. Her mother had fled upstairs, leaving Tilly alone at the counter. The baby had been home just a few days by then, and Tilly still didn't know what it meant. She was nervous but proud of the way she was able to talk to Dunne. She told him Emma had never seen the moon. When Ada came back down, the baby in her arms, Tilly was helping another customer. Dunne had left.

Ada ran to the front of the shop and looked out of the door. "Didn't you tell him to wait?" she cried. "Where did he go?"

"I don't know," Tilly said. "He bought some potatoes."

Ada looked up and down the street. "But didn't you tell him I was coming back down?"

"No."

"Why not?"

"That's not what you said."

"I said I was going to get the baby!"

Backing into the stockroom, Tilly nodded. "Yes."

"But I wanted him to see Paul! Didn't you know that?"

Tilly was strangely still. "Why?" she asked.

Ada froze.

"Why? Why did you want him to see Paul?" Tilly asked, repeating the question again and again, some part of her hoping Ada could surprise her with a different truth. "What happened? What did we do? Why did you want to show him the baby?"

Under the covers Tilly curls on her side and tucks her knees up for warmth. She's cradling a space, a hollow, that she imagines for Emma or Paul. The air grows warm with her breath, and she'd like to fall asleep but can't. She can't forget that she stood in that doorway and refused to accept the greatest thing her mother could do to make amends.

What could her mother say? What had she wanted her to say? That when Raisa had seemed to pause on the steps, she—Yes! They both knew it. She'd let go of Tilly and pushed Raisa, hard, in the back. Raisa had turned as she stumbled. Ada yelled, "Go on!" and—here was the crucial thing—kept moving. Raisa might have caught her balance otherwise. But Ada gave her—this refugee who seemed to know so much—an order and then walked right over her. Anyone could have seen that it pleased her to do so.

But why hadn't Raisa righted herself? Why hadn't everyone proceeded into the station as they always had, safe? How could Ada have known Raisa was carrying a baby? How could she have known what was coming behind?

"What did we do?" Tilly said to her mother. "What did we do?"

"You didn't do anything," Ada finally answered.

Tilly stared, then bolted outside. Ada ran after her until she was out of breath—not far, with the baby in her arms—then called her name, over and over, but Tilly had kept going until she reached the end of the street, rounded the corner, and was gone.

In many ways, she never came back. They lived together half a dozen more years but never spoke of the tragedy again. Never hugged or touched. Tilly clutches her stomach, keening with tears, trying to keep all the sound under the blanket so that she won't wake her boys. Her mum. Her darling mum. By the time Tilly relented and named her second child for Ada's father—the best she could do, having a second boy—her mother was dead. Hadn't Ada just been trying to keep them safe? But that night, that push, whatever it was, had taken away both her girls. Tilly will try to tell Paul in the morning.

That night a storm blows over London, with a surprising amount of snow, and the young people on the phone to their parents and grandparents begin to say good night. They peer out at the city. "Traffic will be slow in the morning."

"Of course. Good night," the old people say. Thunder booms, marking the night for meteorological interest, a perfect cusp between winter and spring.

Do they think the children will remember the story this time around? Not really. Well, perhaps just enough. They open their curtains before going to bed so that light will fill the rooms first thing in the morning. All over London people who lived through the blackout years do the same.

Forty-eight

She was a woman in a crowd, surrounded but alone. When the crowd flowed into the stairwell, she stumbled. Her right knee hit the step, but she kept the baby tight against her left side, her torso upright. With her right hand she groped and was almost up when a body brushing past took her balance and forced her all the way down.

Why did they presume to know how a traumatized person should behave? Their eyes told her she was not doing what they expected, what they wanted. It made her nervous but she could not address it. All her energy went to the baby, to organizing a day around a single errand. That's how much time everything took. She imagined a future after the war, when life might be simpler, but she was not there yet.

She met the pavement with the right side of her body and head, then instinctively curled around the baby and knew that he was fine. In the darkness she heard gasps, groans. Sobs and thuds, one after the other, coming very fast.

Every night she'd used the shelter, she'd watched these people. They were all accustomed to living in close quarters, as was she. She'd seen annoyance, even rage, but time and again the spirit of common dis-advantage took over, and nothing happened. Today, though, she'd felt in the air a potent mixture of worry and exhaustion. Everyone seemed to be moving fast, making mistakes. She'd seen a man on a bicycle nearly hit a child, a woman steal a bag of groceries. Everyone was tired and burdened, unable to absorb any more shock. That afternoon she'd searched in her pocket for something to give the scared child. She had a button, two hairpins, a broken silver earring. The button delighted him, and he added it to the marbles and beads already in his pockets. As the sweet boy walked away, she thought, What happens now?

At the last possible moment, she rolled left and found herself facing the inside of the station, the dim lights of the booking hall. People were running to help, dark shapes against the light, but she knew something terrible was happening. She could not fill her lungs. Anger rose in her, and she bucked and kicked and screamed. The lining of her throat felt scraped raw, but she heard no sound. Hair filled her mouth; wool covered her eyes and nose; something pressing on her head muffled all sound. Terror overwhelmed her, and she stopped fighting and curled around her child. She still could not fill her lungs, but she felt him breathing, stirring, beneath the arm she kept cantilevered over his tiny frame. She was conscious, still, and saw the man who reached for him. She felt his arms. Then people tugged on her hands, her legs, her arms. She heard voices far away and, closer, the choking sound of people trying to breathe, all of them in various states of struggle. It was incredible to her that she had come so far yet could not make it to safety. She closed her eyes and remembered how her baby had felt under her coat these last few winter months. Soft and warm. Hers. The only thing that was, until he wasn't.

Author's Note

I am indebted to a number of books and sources for giving me historical background for this story. *Family and Kinship in East London* by Michael Young and Peter Willmott is a fascinating sociological study of community and family life in Bethnal Green. For a sense of what it was like to live in London during the war, *How We Lived Then* by Norman Longmate and *London at War* by Philip Ziegler were both invaluable. Also, Mary Lee Settle's essay in the *Virginia Quarterly Review*, "London—1944"; Paul Fussell's *Wartime;* and the BBC's WW2 People's War online project were very useful. The shelter drawings of Henry Moore as gathered in Julian Andrews's book *London's War* were provocative and inspiring, and the following books provided useful information about the behaviour of crowds: *Among the Thugs*, Bill Buford; *The Crowd*, Gustave Le Bon; *The Crowd in History*, George Rude; *Panic and Morale: Conference Transactions*, the New York Academy of Medicine and the Josiah Macy Jr. Foundation.

I will be for ever grateful to Her Majesty's Stationery Office in London for making a copy of the report of the original inquiry available to a modern audience as part of the series Uncovered Editions, historical documents not previously available in a popular form. Discovering HMSO's *Tragedy at Bethnal Green* in the bookshop of the British Library one day in 2000 was the start of this story in my mind. Later, Malcolm Barr-Hamilton of the Tower Hamlets Local History Library was helpful in providing me with wartime photographs of the area and newspaper articles about the tragedy, and eventually I read the full historical transcript of the inquiry at the National Archives, Kew Gardens. A crush did happen on the evening of 3 March 1943; news of it was kept secret for days; and a private investigation was ultimately led by a magistrate named Laurence Dunne. The government suppressed his report until after the war. The rest of the story, as I've told it in this book, is fiction.

A plaque in the Bethnal Green Tube station commemorates the incident. It reads:

Site of the worst civilian disaster of the Second World War

In memory of the 173 men, women and children who lost their lives on the evening of Wednesday 3rd March 1943 descending these steps to Bethnal Green underground air raid shelter

Not forgotten

Acknowledgments

This book was written in many libraries: the British Library, the London Library, the University of Virginia Law Library, the Miller Center at the University of Virginia, the Fine Arts Library at the University of Pennsylvania, and Bobst Library at New York University. Thank you to all of these institutions for granting me reading privileges and thus giving me a place to write. A special debt of gratitude to Kent Olson at the University of Virginia for finding me the 1942 map of the Borough of Bethnal Green that I carried with me everywhere I worked on the book.

Fellowships from the MacDowell Colony and the Virginia Center for the Creative Arts came at critical times and were absolutely inspiring. Thank you, also, to all the people who looked after my family when I was away: Claudia and Peter Kane, Ann Canavan, and Linda Ahlen.

I am grateful to all the people who read the book, in some cases several times, and offered indispensable support in the form of conversation and good advice: Rosecrans Baldwin, Rachel Cohen, Liz Darhansoff, Michael Downing, Katie Dublinski, Emmanuelle Ertel, Margaret Hutton Griffin, Elizabeth Kiem, John McNally, and Janice P. Nimura.

My editor, Fiona McCrae, expertly guided this book in its final stages, and it is indescribably better for her attention. I'd also like to thank Laura Barber, my editor at Portobello Books in London. Her early and strong embrace has meant a great deal.

My parents, Anthony and Marion Francis, never doubted that I would one day write a novel, even when I was sure they were mistaken. Their confidence was encouraging, to say the least.

Both of my children, Olivia and Simon, were born during the writing of this book. They may have slowed my pace, but taking care of them taught me what I needed to finish the story. And finally, but actually first and always, Mitchell. He was this book's first reader, and it is dedicated to him with all my love.

The text of *The Report* is set in Adobe Caslon Pro. This typeface was designed by Carol Twombly and is based on William Caslon's original creation, which had characteristics of Dutch Baroque types. Book design by Rachel Holscher.